This book belongs to

Tamsin

Bush

FAMILY PLAYBILL

*It wasn't fair, Lexy told herself for the thousandth time, that she
— a Mannering — should be so plain. Often people would
refuse to believe that she was a Mannering, for the family were
noted throughout the theatrical profession, and beyond it, for
their good looks . . . .*

The Mannerings travelled from town to town, playing a week
here and a week there in grim northern towns like Doncaster
and Leeds and Sheffield, grim indeed in the 1850's. Every
Sunday they downed scenery, packed up costumes and
properties, and journeyed in dirty, smut-laden railway
carriages to their next theatrical venue — where often the
audiences were few and unappreciative.

Apart from Lexy herself (who was reckoned hopeless at
acting and spent most of her time on stage standing still and
holding props), the other Mannerings were her little brother
Clem, whose long golden curls enchanted every audience; her
mother Seraphina who looked like the angel she was named
after; her father Joshua, an impressive actor-manager; Jamie
the baby — and, of course, her older sister Cecily who had
rejoined the company after years at a finishing school.

The theatre was the only life Lexy knew, but to Cecily, it
and the dingy boarding houses in which the actors stayed,
seemed squalid and provincial after the glories of "Miss
Dingwater's Academy for Young Ladies", and she did
everything she could to take as little part in things as possible,
making much extra work and worry for poor Lexy.

Family tensions, petty rivalries, unexpected dangers and all
the richly-patterned life of the Victorian theatre are the
ingredients of this compulsive novel by the author of *The
Swish of the Curtain* and who has herself been on the stage.

BY THE SAME AUTHOR

The Swish of the Curtain
The Finishing School

FAMILY PLAYBILL

PAMELA BROWN

Illustrated by Gavin Rowe

JOHN GOODCHILD PUBLISHERS
AYLESBURY

John Goodchild Publishers
10 Mandeville Road
Aylesbury
Buckinghamshire
HP21 8AA

John Goodchild Publishers is an imprint of Bookward Ltd

First published in this revised edition 1986
© Copyright Pamela Brown 1951, 1986
Illustrations © Copyright Gavin Rowe 1980

All rights reserved. No part of this publication may be reproduced, stored in a retrieval system, or transmitted in any form or by any means, electronic, mechanical, photocopying, recording or otherwise without the prior written permission of the publishers.

Cover illustration by Gordon King
Cover lettering by Susan Harris

Set in 11 on 14pt Times by Input Typesetting Ltd of London. Printed by Nene Litho and bound by Woolnough Bookbinding Ltd both of Irthlingborough, Northants.

British Library Cataloguing in Publication Data
Brown, Pamela, 1924 —
    Family Playbill—New ed.
    I. Title
    823' .912 [J]   PZ7

ISBN 0-86391-093-9

FOR
MY MOTHER AND FATHER
WITH LOVE

CONTENTS

CHAPTER 1

A Finished Young Lady

As soon as Lexy opened her eyes she knew what day it was. She knew by the curling rags that twisted her hair into uncomfortable knots on which she had tossed and turned all night. It was Sunday. Next she began to wonder what town they were in. Doncaster? Leeds? Sheffield? No, of course, that was last week – Braddersfield – that was it – they were at Braddersfield at Mrs Thirkett's; she recognised the lamp brackets. And today they were to travel to – Suddenly Lexy shot upright in the big bed, disturbing little Clemence who was asleep beside her. He whined and burrowed deeper into the pillow.

"Clem – Clem – " she cried and shook him by the shoulder. "Wake up – "

"Shan't – " he answered, and kicked her sleepily.

Lexy sighed and looked down at his tumbled golden curls and dark sweeping lashes. When he was asleep he looked angelic, but she knew only too well to what extent his devilment could reach during every waking moment.

"But Clem," she persisted, in an urgent whisper, "don't you realise – it's today we're going to Oldcastle, and

Cecily's joining us at Turnpike Junction! You want to see your sister, don't you?"

"Silly old sister!" Clem pretended to snore to show how little interested he was, but Lexy knew that he too had suddenly felt excited when he realised that today they were to see the sister whom he had never seen before – whom Lexy hadn't seen for six years.

Lexy steeled herself for getting out of bed. The bare boards were as cold as she had feared, and she shivered as she ran over to the mirror. This she did every morning in the hope that one day she would look at her reflection and find that she had suddenly grown beautiful overnight. But this morning it was the same as always – slightly worse because of the curling rags. She looked coldly at her mouse-coloured hair, cut in a fringe, at her pale face, and slightly protruding front teeth. Mechanically she covered them with her lips, hearing in her mind the ever-repeated words of her mother: "Cover your teeth up, Lexy."

It wasn't fair, she told herself for the thousandth time, that she – a Mannering – should be so plain. Often people would refuse to believe that she *was* a Mannering, for the family were noted throughout the theatrical profession, and beyond it, for their good looks. She glanced across at the other big bed in the low attic room. Even wearing their night-caps her parents looked well. She walked over to the bed and peeped at them. "Seraphina Mannering" – she said her mother's name over to herself as she looked down at her. She thought it the most beautiful name in the world. Seraphina – a seraph was a sort of angel, wasn't it? She had heard it in church on the rare occasions when they had not been travelling on a Sunday and were able to go. And that's just what her mother looked like –

a seraph – thought Lexy, and that was where Clem got his looks from. They both had the same broad clear brow, honey-coloured hair, and those blue eyes that dazzled you when they were open. There were a few lines now under her eyes and at the corners of her mouth, but Lexy thought they were beautiful, too.

Her father murmured in his sleep and she turned to look at him. He had luxuriant brown hair that showed beneath his striped night-cap in a gallant forelock. Lexy felt glad that her father was clean-shaven. Everyone had beards or whiskers or moustaches now except actors and even some actors had them. Even though he was asleep, his features were composed and noble, and Lexy feared that at any moment he would open his eyes and say, "You see, me dear – like that – relaxed and calm as though you were asleep," as he did when he tried to teach her to stand still on the stage and not to cough or twitch or shuffle her feet. Lexy spent a lot of her life standing still on the stage. That was the reason for the fringe. In nearly every production in the Mannerings' repertoire, Lexy played a page, and stood holding things. In "The Merchant of Venice" she held a basket of doves, in "Romeo and Juliet" she held someone's train, in "Julius Caesar" she held a scroll – and so on.

If there were any really good parts for children, Clem played them. Already, at six, he was an experienced actor, having played many parts since he was four. His triumphs were Arthur in "King John", Mamillius in "The Winter's Tale", and little Sir Randolph in one of the melodramas. He learned his lines parrot-fashion from his father and never forgot them. But not even Joshua Mannering – one of the most famous actor-managers of the Northern Circuit – could teach his son to put any expression into the lines. But the

11

audience did not mind. As soon as Clem entered with his blond curls hanging almost to his shoulders, and his angelic countenance, there were murmurs of "Oh, the mite!" and "Clever little soul!" before he even opened his mouth. Not that Lexy was envious. She was only too glad not to have the work of learning lines, as she had done before Clem was old enough to play. It was one of the only good things about not being pretty.

Then baby Jamie started to cry, and the day had really begun. Jamie slept in a wicker basket with two handles by the side of his parents' bed at night, and in fact nearly all the time. He slept in it in trains, in coaches, in theatre dressing-rooms, and sometimes, during rehearsals, actually in the wings, so that his mother could keep her eye on him. He was only a few months old and Lexy could not feel very strongly about him. He wasn't a personality like Clem. He was a pretty baby and moderately good, but he made so much more work, mainly for Lexy. She picked him up and rocked him for a few minutes, shivering under her voluminous calico nightdress. His crying had woken up his mother.

"Lexy, child," she said sleepily, stretching like a beautiful marmalade cat, "run to Mrs Thirkett for the hot water – I'll take the little man."

Jamie was deposited in bed with his parents, and Lexy pulled on her thick travelling cloak, and a pair of old dancing slippers and padded down through the tall, cold, silent house. In the basement there were sounds of activity. Mrs Thirkett and the skinny maid-of-all-work were preparing the breakfast, judging by the smell of bacon cooking.

"Ee, luv, yer've coom for 'ot water, I'll be bound,"

said Mrs Thirkett loudly, when she saw Lexy. She was fat and always red-cheeked but even more so now, from bending over the kitchen range. Lexy could never get used to the northern brogue, however much they travelled round these parts. The diction and elocution of her mother and father were always so perfect that she could not understand how other people could produce such strange and varied sounds.

"See that there lazy Ma and Pa o' your'n don't keep breakfast waiting, lass," said Mrs Thirkett, handing her the heavy earthenware pitcher full of hot water. As she carried it up the stairs Lexy pitied the maid, who was not much more than her own twelve years, and who fetched and carried up the steep stairs for sixteen hours a day.

In the bedroom the morning was beginning badly. Clem lay kicking on the bed shouting "Shan't" to everything that he was told to do, Jamie was still crying, her mother was complaining of a headache and Joshua was storming because there was no clean linen for him. They washed in turn at the large cracked bowl – Lexy put on her chemise, drawers and petticoats, and then dressed the baby, while her mother dressed Clem.

"Mrs Thirkett says we're not to keep breakfast, Mamma," said Lexy.

"Indeed we shall not," said her father in his deep resonant bass. "We shall descend with all good speed – "

"That we must, if we're to catch the train!" cried Mrs Mannering, floating round the room in a silk negligee much too thin for the winter. "Oh, to think of seeing my child again – my ewe lamb." She dabbed her eyes with a handkerchief.

13

"She's not your ewe lamb, mamma," Lexy corrected her, "not actually – "

"But I've not seen the child for six years, Lexy – Spring 1851 she went off to school and this is 1857. Just think of that – six years – it's a long time for a mother to be parted from her child."

"Yes, Mamma – but would you please get dressed – otherwise we'll miss the train and you'll not see her even now."

As usual the actual organising of getting everyone down to breakfast was left to Lexy. She combed Clem's sausage curls round her fingers so that they fell in lovely natural clusters and she struggled with her own crimped frizz that would not go into proper ringlets. She knew that it became her much better during the week when it hung completely straight to her shoulders, but it was considered part of Sunday for Lexy's hair to be curled.

"Though we may not be able to worship on the Sabbath, at least we can honour it," as her father said, and on Sundays he invariably put on his best clothes even if it was only to travel in dirty railway carriages. Lexy always thought that he looked very splendid in his long black cloak and top hat and the cravat that he always wore although it was out of date. And today being an extra special Sunday, they had all to put on their very best. As Lexy struggled into her tartan dresss with the little white collar she wished that it were not so shabby. Two years ago when it had been new she had been so proud of it and thought it very fashionable. But now it hardly seemed good enough for going to meet a sister who had been six years at a finishing school.

Lexy wondered just how finished Cecily would be –

she supposed it meant that her sister would have learned so much that there was nothing more for her to be taught. Lexy had never been to school at all. It was supposed that her father taught her, and so he did – but not the usual school subjects of reading, writing and arithmetic. He taught her to form her vowels beautifully.

"So that they fall from your mouth like jewels," he would say. And by this time she knew by heart a good dozen plays of Shakespeare, merely by hearing her father's lines for him. She knew the towns of northern England as well as most girls know their own back yards, and though she may not have known what their chief products were, she could say in which street were the cheapest lodgings and whether the theatre dressing-rooms were good. From her mother she had learnt how to apply a stage make-up, and the cheapest joints to ask for at the butcher's. Those were the only two practical things she had learnt from her mother. All the other things Lexy had heard from her were romantic stories of her youth when she had been a dancer in burlesque in London and peers of the realm had thronged at the stage-door to see her and artists had clamoured to paint her, and there had been flowers and champagne and gay supper parties. Seraphina's face would light up as she described it all to her grave-eyed daughter.

"And what happened then, Mamma?" Lexy would ask.

"Then I married your father – " And Seraphina would return to the present and the pile of mending which never got done, the difficult classical lines to learn that she never really understood, and the never-ending journeys.

At last they were ready to go down to breakfast.

"Come, let us go," said Joshua, and led the way with

Seraphina following, holding Clem's hand and Lexy carrying Jamie.

Down in the basement, they sat round the kitchen table with Mrs Thirkett, and the maid served their breakfast. It was warm and cosy in the kitchen and Lexy wished they hadn't to go on the long train journey. They ate gruel, bacon and eggs. Joshua had kidney with his as well and a pint of porter. Seraphina and Lexy drank tea and the little ones had milk. When they had finished, Joshua leaned back in his chair.

"And now Mrs Thirkett, our little account with you."

Promptly Mrs Thirkett produced from the detachable pocket that hung round her waist a long bill for their weekly stay with her. Lexy looked anxiously at her father. Sometimes when it had been a bad week, Joshua found fault with the bill and refused to pay so much and there were angry scenes in which the words "rogues and vagabonds" and "Never again will a play-actor set foot across my threshold" were apt to figure rather largely. But this week all was well and Joshua produced a sovereign and some coppers and laid them on the table.

"With gratitude, dear lady, for our pleasant sojourn with you," he said.

Mrs Thirkett bobbed and smiled and swept the money into her pocket.

"Ee, it's a pleasure to 'ave you, that it is, sir," she said. "I 'ope to see you back soon."

"That you shall, good lady," said Joshua. "As soon as kindly fate shall lead us hither. Come, little ones," and with a gesture straight out of "Little Sir Randolph" he ushered his flock from the room.

Now came the very worst time of Sunday – the

packing up. A certain amount of their belongings had gone with the theatre baggage but there was all their personal luggage to be packed into trunks and wooden boxes and strapped up. Lexy did most of this with Clem hindering her. He kept remembering things that he wanted which were right at the bottom of trunks she had strapped up. Seraphina was re-doing her lovely hair in front of the mirror, so that it came smoothly from the centre parting, draped round her ears and formed a large plaited bun in a net at the back of her head. As she did this she regretted aloud the fact that nowadays she had to do her own hair with no help from a maid or a dresser.

"Just a minute, Mamma, I'm coming to help you," said Lexy as she bounced on a trunk to close it. Her father had gone out to fetch a cab and when he arrived with one, there was the usual last-minute flurry because Clem had lost a mitten and all the baby's clean napkins had been packed. At last they were in the cab and Mrs Thirkett was waving to them with her apron from the doorstep. As they trotted along to the station, Lexy was glad that it would be a first-class journey and not third-class. For the third-class carriages on this line were still of the open cattle-truck type, and after a bad week, the long cold journey with dust and bits of coke flying into their eyes, was a cruel experience with two small children, wrapped as they might be in travelling rugs and cloaks. The first-class carriages at least were covered in, though the seats were hard, and the windows small. When they bought the tickets the clerk looked suspiciously at Lexy.

"You've no need to strain your eyes, my man," said Seraphina. "She's as much under twelve as you're over it." And Lexy's half-price ticket was bought.

On the platform they joined up with the rest of Mr Mannering's company. First there were Mr and Mrs Tollerton, the heavy character man and woman. Matthew Tollerton was small and screwed up with a face wrinkled like a walnut shell. He wore steel-rimmed spectacles through which he frowned frighteningly and Lexy thought that he looked just like Scrooge in Mr Charles Dickens's tale, "A Christmas Carol". His wife, Gertrude, was enormously fat, which was very useful for comedy parts, but she was so fat that she often made people laugh when she went on in more serious rôles. But Lexy thought that as the Nurse in "Romeo and Juliet" she made her both laugh and cry more than any other actress she had ever seen. Lexy adored her because she never made remarks about Ugly Ducklings and things like that, as other members of the company did.

With them was Barney Fidgett, one of the "utility" men who played any small part that was going or just walked on. He was very old, with a soft fringe of white hair round the sides of his bald head, and was very useful for playing imposing old men as long as they had few lines or none at all. From being a well-known London actor he had descended to being "general utility" in a touring company as his memory had begun to fail him. Once when Joshua had been taken ill, Mr Fidgett had had to go on to play "Lear" which he had played many times before, but when his first cue came he had dried completely, with his mouth wide open in surprise. Someone had thrust the book into his hands and he had read the whole part, with tears of humiliation in his gentle blue eyes.

A little apart along the platform stood Courtney Stanton, the juvenile lead, a handsome young man, tall and rather willowy with fair hair and a profile of which he was always careful to give the audience the full benefit. He was not a good actor but had quite a following in the provincial towns that they visited. Mr Mannering could not stand him, but put up with him because he knew that he attracted a section of the female public that did not care particularly for Shakespeare but liked actors.

The rest of the company were standing in twos and threes along the platform, heavily wrapped in every muffler they could lay hands on. At last the train came in with much puffing and blowing of steam, and the Mannerings found a carriage to themselves. Their luggage was piled on top of the carriage and covered with a tarpaulin by the guard. And then they were off. It was a good two hours' journey to Turnpike Junction, where they were to change, and Lexy was quite glad of a chance to sit still and think; she had so little opportunity usually. She hoped her father would not want her to hear his lines and that Clem would not want her to play cat's cradle. At last there was time to think about Cecily. Cecily – six years ago she had been the age that Lexy was now – She had been pretty, Lexy remembered, but very tomboyish and always getting into trouble for playing jokes on the company. She remembered how Cecily had once put a mouse in the high boots that Mr Tollerton wore and he had slipped them on just before his cue came and not noticed the mouse until he had got on the stage. Lexy giggled to herself. What fun it would be to have Cecily back again!

"Pray share the joke," said her father, who sat opposite.

"I was just thinking, Papa, how glad I shall be to have Cecily with us again."

"Ah, yes – it will be a joy to see the family complete

once more. And it will save the trouble of looking for another juvenile girl. They're always a nuisance – they become engaged to be married and have fits of the vapours, or else they *don't* become engaged to be married, and have fits of the vapours."

"I shall be glad to have my darling daughter back," said Mrs Mannering, with a sigh, "not only for her dear company but so that I need no longer play these parts of slips of girls that I am much too old for."

"Nonsense, my precious."

"Of course you're not too old, Mamma," chorused Lexy and her father. Clem looked at his mother with critical blue eye eyes.

"Yes, Mamma, you do look more like a mamma than a girl, you know," he said candidly.

"Oh, it's this bonnet, no doubt." Seraphina tried to catch her reflection in the window. "I always felt it was a little too elderly. Perhaps with a plume or two – "

"At all events," continued Joshua, "Cecily will relieve your mother of many a burden, both in the theatre and domestically."

"Me too," thought Lexy. "She'll be able to help with the little ones."

"But will she have forgotten all about acting, I wonder?" she said aloud.

"Never!" cried Joshua. "As a child she was an excellent little trouper. Never knew the meaning of the word 'nerves'. She was as hardy as a boy. And she knew how to stand still during other people's scenes."

Lexy flushed at this dig at herself, but she did not try to explain that sometimes her arms ached so from holding the spear or trumpet or whatever it was, that she just *had* to move, even though it might be in the middle of her father's best speech.

As they sped through the grim little northern towns at quite fifteen miles an hour, Lexy marvelled at the wonders of modern travel. In some parts of the country one still had to travel by coach, and although she loved the gaily-painted vehicles with two horses, she was still exited by to the miracle of getting up in Braddersfield, taking a train and going to bed in Oldcastle.

Then she watched the lights in the windows of the houses they passed. As it was still quite early in the morning and the sky was heavy and overcast, the lamps were alight in most of them. Lexy caught glimpses of families sitting down to breakfast, a little girl playing with a dog in a garden, people on their way to church clasping prayer books. How strange, she thought, to live in the same place all the time. The Mannerings had never had a home of their own. There was that time when Papa had been in the stock company at Manchester, and they had stayed there two years, but even then they had changed their lodgings three times for some reason or another. Lexy felt a slight envy and a somewhat superior feeling for the young girls who lived in the same house all the time and went to school and never stepped inside a theatre. Then all the houses and the green fields and the mills and the mines and the railway sidings began to merge into one long blurred strip moving continually past the window, and Lexy slept until suddenly a porter shouted loudly, "Turnpike Junction!" And Lexy jumped up to help Clem on with his mittens, rearrange the baby's basket, and help her mother to find her reticule.

Turnpike Junction was not a town, it was merely the connecting point of two branches of the railway, but as it

21

was situated in the centre of some of the most important northern manufacturing towns, a lot of traffic passed through it, and on Sundays the station platform was a rendezvous for the touring theatrical companies. The Mannerings seemed to spend some time there almost every Sunday. The woman who worked behind the refreshment counter in the buffet was a retired dancer who had been in the chorus at the Royalty Theatre when Seraphina had been the première danseuse, and they loved to get together and have a chat about old times, and who had been passing through the junction lately and with what company. She always produced some extra tit-bit for the children other than the food displayed on the counter. But today they had no thought of the refreshment-room until they had found Cecily.

"Shall we recognise her, Mamma?" said Lexy anxiously. "Will she have changed?"

"I trust so," said her mother, "otherwise the scraping and saving we have done to keep her at school will have been a waste, now won't it? But I shall know my daughter, however changed she may be."

"Where are we meeting her, my precious? Under the clock? I see no one resembling her – " Joshua strode on ahead up the platform, his cloak flying out behind him so that a lot of people turned to stare.

"There go the theatricals – " someone whispered.

Lexy always thought that as a family they looked quite ordinary, until they found themselves amongst other people. And then there always seemed to be something that set them apart. Was it the loud resonance of her father's voice, or her mother's faded beauty? Although Seraphina never wore make-up off-stage, somehow the colour of her stage make-up seemed to be a permanency and her lips and cheeks were redder and her eyes more lively than any other woman's.

Along the draughty platform they trailed. Everything was grey and covered with soot and smuts. There were not many travellers about. They were mainly huddled over the meagre fire in the waiting-room or drinking hot soup at the buffet.

Under the clock there was no young girl waiting. Only a very fine lady in a fur tippet and a much be-feathered hat, who held one side of her voluminous crinoline skirt fastidiously away from the dirty platform.

"Cripes, look at that," said Clem vulgarly, but his mother and father were staring too fixedly at the lady to remonstrate with him.

"No, Seraphina – " said Joshua, incredulously.

"Yes, Joshua, yes – it is – I think – " Seraphina advanced slowly towards her, and said timidly, "Miss Mannering?"

The vision turned wide blue eyes on her – Mannering eyes – and the rosebud mouth opened into a dainty affected O.

"Oh, Mamma – it is weally you?" Cecily kissed her lightly on each cheek. "I can't believe it – you've altered so – I wemember you as young and lovely."

Seraphina, rather taken aback, released her daughter from a large embrace.

"And Papa," she trilled. "A kiss for you too, Papa." Her lips hardly touched her father's cheek.

"And this is never Lexy – oh, what a pity – what a shame about her teeth, Mamma," she said loudly.

Lexy blushed, imagining that everyone on the platform had heard the remark.

23

"And Clemence – my little lamb!" She picked up her brother and kissed him. "Now you are weally a lovely boy."

Clem looked at her steadily: "Mamma, why does she talk so funnily?" he enquired.

"Oh, Cecily, my dear, we are so glad to welcome you back," Seraphina went on, ignoring Clem. "But you haven't seen little Jamie – " She indicated the basket that Lexy had set down. Cecily raised her beautifully gloved hands in a gesture of horror.

"Oh, no, I don't care for babies. Please don't ask me to hold him. I should scweam." Lexy's heart sank. "However, I'll take a look at him if you wish. He *is* my bwother, although the child of your old age, Mamma."

When the covers were turned back she just said, "Oh, yes. He favours the Mannerings, which is a welief after Alexandwa here. Child, what have you done to your hair?" she asked her.

"Curled it," said Lexy miserably.

"Did you damp the wags?"

"Come, children," said Joshua, "I see no reason why we should stand braving the inclement weather in this way. Let us partake of some refreshment. You must be starved, daughter, after your journey from the south. Have you travelled through the night?"

"Oh, no, Papa, I stayed with fwiends at Buxton last night. The Honouwable Poppy Pagett, you know, who was my bosom fwiend at the Misses Dingwaters'."

"Oh yes, I have heard tell of her from your letters. They are wealthy people, I believe."

"Oh yes, Papa. But then all the girls at the Misses Dingwaters' were cawwiage folk."

In the refreshment-room Cecily refused to sit down

at any of the benches for fear of soiling her gown, and turned up her nose at the hot grog, the whelks and eels and meat pies that were for sale.

"Weally, I hardly eat enough to keep a spawwow alive."

"Well, that's one good thing," thought Lexy, who had been the only one to realise that now they would have an extra mouth to feed. But eventually Cecily managed to consume three jam puffs that would have kept a whole family of sparrows alive for some time.

"How long do we have to wait for the twain to take us to – oh, what is the name of the howwid place?"

"Oldcastle. We have three quarters of an hour," said Joshua.

"Then, Papa," said Cecily, "let us talk about my future."

Her father looked at her blankly. "Your future? What of it?"

"Well – what am I to do?"

"Juliet, Ophelia, Desdemona, for a certainty, and then perhaps some of the heavier parts, oh and of course all the ingénués in the dramas and a few comedy parts in the curtain-raisers."

Cecily's mouth dropped open. "*Me!* I am to *play-act* – with the west of you?"

"But of course," said Joshua blankly. "What else should you do?"

Cecily's eyes swam with tears.

"Then why did you send me to the Misses Dingwaters' if I am not to be a lady? I don't wish to join the twoupe again. I should like to go into Society. The Pagetts are willing to pwesent me at Court – "

"The only Court you will see, me girl, is the Court Theatre, Oldcastle. Now let's have no more of this tara-diddle. We need a new juvenile girl, and you are to be she. It is time you took your rightful place in the company. The more we keep it in the family, the less do we pay out in salaries. You will receive fifteen shillings a week, and your keep, which is princely for a girl of your age, is it not, Mamma?"

Seraphina nodded. Lexy could see that she was hurt at Cecily not wishing to stay with them.

"But – but I spend more than that on bonnets alone," cried Cecily horrified.

"And out of the fifteen shillings you will have to provide a great deal of your own costumes for the stage," continued her father implacably. "Now let us hear no more of it."

Cecily's lip trembled. Lexy took hold of her hand and squeezed it sympathetically.

"You won't mind it when you get used to it, Cecily," she said. "We used to enjoy ourselves. Do you remember Mr Tollerton and the mouse?"

"Who? What mouse?" And Lexy saw that her sister's childhood had fallen away from her as though she had never lived it.

And then Seraphina had to introduce Cecily to her friend behind the refreshment bar and, although Cecily was very dignified and patronising, the open admiration that she received put her into a good temper again, and she chattered away about her life at the Misses Dingwaters' Academy for Young Ladies.

Then it was time for them to get on to the train for Oldcastle. As the company re-assembled, Cecily was introduced to all of them, and blushed and simpered prettily. Courtney Stanton bowed very low, and said, "Your servant, ma'moiselle," which pleased Cecily greatly. Mr Tollerton said, "Ah, yes, I remember you!" in a baleful tone that made Lexy bend over Jamie's basket in order to hide her smile.

"Oh, how I do dislike these howwid twain journeys!" said Cecily as they got into the carriage.

"You will soon become accustomed to them, daughter," said Joshua, "for we travel every week, occasionally three times or more."

Cecily turned pale, and, producing a tiny bottle of smelling-salts from her reticule, she inhaled them delicately.

"And how long shall we be at Oldcastle?" she enquired.

"A week. We play a different piece each night, beginning with 'The Merchant of Venice' tomorrow night. Would you care to walk on as a lady-in-waiting?"

"Oh, no, Papa, please. I would wather watch. I wemember your Shylock fwom when I was little."

Joshua was pleased.

"Of course you shall watch, me child. I'll see that you have a box all to yourself."

They arrived at Oldcastle in the late afternoon. On the platform was a cluster of landladies who had come to look for lodgers for the ensuing week.

"Oh, deary me!" said Seraphina. "There's that unpleasant Mrs Hodges! Do you remember? We had some little trouble with her over the bill when we were here before. Look the other way, children."

All around them members of the company were saying firmly to the landladies, "No, no. That's far too much! Why, I know of lodgings in the next street to you that are half-a-crown cheaper."

A weedy looking gentleman in a black coat that was almost green with age stepped up to the Mannerings.

"Seeing as the Missus is poorly, she sent me to say as would you and yours, Mr Mannering, do us the honour of gracing our 'umble abode – at very reduced terms for the profession."

With the well-remembered Mrs Hodges casting menacing glances at them, they went off with this gentleman and found a cab. Somehow the addition of Cecily made everything much more complicated. There were all her piles of luggage to add to their own, and she made no effort to carry anything herself, and whenever anyone else picked up a case of hers, she would say, "Oh pway take care. That has my cut-glass hair-tidy in it," or "That one has my jewellery – be vewy careful."

She whispered to her mother: "Mamma, must we weally go with this howwid common man? Why cannot we go to an hotel?"

"Because of the tariff," said Seraphina bluntly. "You seem to have forgotten all your experience of touring as a child."

"I have twied to," Cecily grimaced, and Seraphina looked so hurt that Lexy could have kicked her sister.

When they arrived at the lodgings and the cab stopped, even Lexy was appalled. It was a small house in a narrow squalid street, black with the smoke of the factories, and dirty children were playing barefooted in the gutters. Cecily resorted to her smelling-salts again. When the land-lord got out of the cab to open the front door, she said urgently, "Father, tell him that we cannot stay here. We

28

can find more suitable apartments than this. Wemember, Papa, you are a well-known actor – "

"Well-known, perhaps, but needy, I'm afraid, me child. You must resign yourself to a more humble mode of existence than has been your lot in recent years."

"Perhaps it will be nice inside," said Lexy comfortingly, picking up Clem who was fast asleep, and carrying him on to the doorstep. But it was not. There were two rooms vacant. The one that Mr and Mrs Mannering took had a truckle-bed for Clem, and Lexy and Cecily had a long narrow slip of a room where the large iron bedstead left hardly enough space for the girls to get in.

"No dwessing-table," mourned Cecily. "How shall I do my toilet?"

"Borrow Mamma's make-up box. There's a mirror in the top of that," suggested Lexy.

29

"But I need a *long* miwwor!"

Lexy struggled with her own unpacking and Cecily's – not that there was anywhere to put anything – and then went in to help her mother with Jamie. Their supper was meagre in the extreme. A thin watery broth, followed by some small steaks and badly-cooked vegetables. Cecily left most of hers, looking doubtfully at the dirty hands of the landlady's husband who served it. There was nowhere to sit afterwards but in Mr and Mrs Mannering's room, where they had to be very quiet, as the two little ones were asleep. Lexy and her mother stitched away, renovating one of the dresses for "The Merchant of Venice", while Joshua went over his lines as Shylock, in a low voice that gradually grew louder as he got more and more into his part.

"Hush, my precious," Seraphina would say at intervals.

Lexy had to work close over her sewing, for there was no lamp in the room – only one candle. Her eyes ached from the close work, and she was stiff from the hours in the railway carriage. Cecily yawned and nodded over a novel, and Clem stirred restlessly in his sleep.

"And now," said Joshua, at ten o'clock, rising and loosening his cravat, "to bed – to sleep – perchance to dream – "

And Sunday was over.

CHAPTER 2

Black Monday

At seven o'clock the next morning, Cecily said sleepily to Lexy, "Bwing me my bweakfast up here, there's a dear girl. I am weally tewwibly tired after that *dweadful* journey." And so, after the usual dressing and washing battle with Clem, there was Cecily's tray to be brought up and numerous trips up and down the rickety stairs because she had forgotten the salt, or a teaspoon, or to see if her sister needed another cup of tea.

These lodgings were very much worse than Mrs Thirkett's at Braddersfield. Rats and mice had disturbed their sleep during the night and there were cockroaches in the kitchen. The landlady was still "poorly" and her husband slopped around in carpet slippers and shirt-sleeves trying to manage the household. The other lodgers all seemed to be morose and bad-tempered at breakfast which was eaten in a Monday-morning-ish silence, and they looked rather askance at the Mannerings for being play-actors.

Rehearsal was to be at ten o'clock as usual, but at nine-thirty Cecily was still in bed. Lexy went to tell her what the time was.

31

"But I don't have to wehearse today. Papa said I need only watch tonight."

"Don't you remember," said Lexy, "we rehearse in the afternoon for the evening's show. In the morning, we work on new pieces that are going into the bill. So you will be needed."

Grumbling, Cecily got out of bed, shivering in her ruffled night-gown. Lexy fetched her hot water, and helped her with her hair, but even then she was not ready by ten o'clock, and by the time she was, the others had started off for the theatre long ago. Fortunately the Court Theatre was very near and they set out to walk there through the dirty streets, with Cecily holding her gown up daintily and picking her way over the muddy crossings. Urchins stopped to stare at her in her large hat which was so fashionable that its like had not yet been seen in Oldcastle.

The Court Theatre was not very big and the outside was somewhat dilapidated but Lexy remembered that inside it was rather nice, with a pleasant green-room and quite good dressing-rooms. Cecily made to go in through the front entrance of the theatre.

"No, no," Lexy stopped her, wondering at her forgetting everything so completely, and led her down the dark, secret little alley in which the stage-door was situated.

It was always when Lexy stepped into the theatre at whatever town they were playing, that she felt at home – never at the lodgings, however often they returned to the same ones. The dusty smell, the litter of scenery being painted and the beehive-like activity reassured her this morning as usual.

"You're late," said Joshua, as they walked on to the stage, accusingly as though they were not his daughters.

"I'm sorry, sir," said Lexy meekly.

"But, Papa – " began Cecily. Then she was cut short by Joshua's brisk, "Now, ladies and gentlemen, to work – "

The prompter handed out scripts of a new burlesque that they were to rehearse that morning, which was being put into the bill the following week. It was called "The Clown's Revenge, or Honesty, the best Policy". And Cecily was to play the heroine in it. All the female members of the company were looking admiringly at her fashionable gown and at the hat which she did not remove, so that the plumes waved in the face of anyone who went near her.

"What an asset to the company – so very ladylike," Courtney Stanton was heard to remark.

But when she started to read, their faces fell. She was hardly audible across the other side of the stage and what with her affected lisp, and the way in which she held her lips pursed, scarcely opening them at all, not a word was audible from the other side of the footlights.

"Cecily," roared Joshua, "what has become of your diction? Cannot you sound your Rs? You used to be able to."

"At the Misses Dingwaters' it was considered vulgar to woll your Rs. They told me I sounded like a stweet-performer."

"And why do you not open your mouth?"

"At the Misses Dingwaters' we were taught to say, 'Pwunes and Pwisms" sixty times evewy morning.'

Joshua roared with disgust, "Prunes and Prisms – to perdition with your prunes and prisms – I want some sound, some *vowels*!" He rolled the words thunderously. And Cecily sniffed irritably and started all over again, this time as though she had a plum in her mouth. The company tittered behind their hands. Lexy blushed for Cecily and buried her face in her script. She was playing the part of a messenger boy with one line – "Yes, sir." At least she could not go far wrong with that.

When it came to a lot of comedy business between Cecily and Mr Tollerton, Joshua said, "Now, put your script down, if you please, and we'll work out this business. First of all, Cecily, you push Mr Tollerton and he falls over. As you fall, Matthew, you push her and she falls too. Now, let us try that."

Cecily blanched. "Papa – must I weally? Today? Now? On this dirty stage? I shall wuin my new gown and I shall bwuise myself."

"Not if you fall properly. Well then, leave it for the present. And in future don't wear your best clothes for rehearsals. Keep them for the show."

While she was waiting for her one entrance, Lexy was bustling around the theatre, helping to get the costumes unpacked from the big wicker skips, heating flat-irons on the coke stove in the stage-door-keeper's office and ironing her mother's robes for Portia that night. Then she set out her mother's and father's make-up boxes in the best dressing-room with the enormous gilt-framed mirror. Jamie was sleeping peacefully in his basket on one end of the dressing-table. Clem, too, was to dress in here, but the two girls were to share a small dressing-room next door. This was a step up for Lexy, for until now she had always put on her costume in the wardrobe-room and made her face up and done her hair in the mirror of anyone who would allow her to peep.

Just as she was setting out her mother's jewel box, fingering lovingly all the large heavy pieces of jewellery,

34

most of them only made of paste and glass but dazzlingly effective across the footlights, Clem came running in shouting gleefully,"You're on. They're calling for you." Lexy flew on to the stage. Joshua, white with rage, was standing in the orchestra pit.

"Is it not enough," he said quietly, "that I have one daughter with impedimented speech? Must I also suffer a half-wit?"

Lexy was in such a fluster that she had left her script in the dressing-room and didn't know from which side she should enter.

"You enter from the left," her father told her slowly and sarcastically, "and you hand the envelope to Mr Tollerton. When he says, 'Is this from the Countess of Marblethorpe?' you say, 'Yes, sir.' Is that clear?"

"Yes, sir," said Lexy and did it.

"Brilliant," said her father. "I trust you will remember your lines."

At lunch-time there was only half an hour's break, and they all went across to a pie-shop opposite the theatre. Lexy loved it here. It was so warm and steamy and cosy, and the pies smelt so delicious. They were only a penny each, and two of them made her feel so full that she had to loosen the sash of her dress. The shop was crowded with working-people – bricklayers, factory hands, mill-workers – and Cecily turned up her pretty nose and applied her smelling-salts.

"It's so close," she murmured, "I feel quite faint."

"Go outside and walk around a bit in the air, then," said her father, but Cecily made no effort to go out in the cold.

The company always seemed particularly friendly at

lunch-time, and exchanged notes on their lodgings and landladies.

"Ah, yes," said Joshua to the Tollertons. "You are at Mrs. Hodges'. A shrew of a woman. If she tells you aught of myself, never believe it."

"She has already spoken of you," said Mrs Tollerton, laughing. "But we took it with a pinch of salt."

"And take care when she presents you with your account, my friends," Joshua warned them. "Oh, yes, a shrew of a woman."

In the afternoon, they went straight through "The Merchant of Venice" in readiness for the evening's performance. Lexy played a page at Portia's court, and Clem played a black servant of the Prince of Morocco. He always got a round of applause when he came on, with his little blackened face and gold turban. The rehearsal went through very quickly as everyone knew the play thoroughly, and they had played it the week before at Braddersfield. Joshua had locked Cecily into her dressing-room and told her that she would not be released until she knew her lines for the burlesque which he was anxious to get into the bill as soon as possible.

Just before they started on the last act, the manager of the theatre came on to the stage looking rather worried.

"How are the bookings?" enquired Joshua.

The manager shook his head gloomily. "There are none," he said.

"*None*?" Joshua was incredulous.

"They don't care much for Shakespeare in Oldcastle, you know, Mr Mannering," the manager said.

"More shame to them," cried Joshua. "But never

fear – those who do come shall enjoy it and spread word of it."

"I hope so. I'm sure I hope so, sir," said the manager gloomily. "Oh yes, Mr Mannering, we have sold one box. And that's a mercy, I'll admit."

"Ah well!" said Joshua. "We are sure of at least a few patrons then."

They went back to the lodgings for tea and ate hungrily of shrimps and celery, and a rather peculiar-tasting caraway-seed cake. Before the show Seraphina always lay down for an hour, and insisted on Clem doing the same. Lexy was considered too young and too old to need a rest and so she finished sewing her mother's dress and heard Cecily's lines, which she did not seem to know at all.

"Then what were you doing all the afternoon, Cecily?" Lexy enquired.

"I was twying a new style of coiffure," Cecily confessed. "Tell me, my dear, do you consider that winglets might still suit me, or do they spoil the line of my pwofile?"

"Cecily, your part!" urged Lexy. "You won't know it by tomorrow!"

"Oh, silly old lines. I can't be bothered with them. I thought I'd finished with learning, now I've left school. I'll make them up as I go along. They're silly and vulgar anyhow."

Lexy had to admit that it was not a very funny comedy.

Then it was time to set off for the theatre again, through the cold darkness. They walked along in procession, Mr and Mrs Mannering in front, carrying Jamie in his basket, then Lexy and Cecily with a sleepy Clem between them, dragging his feet and complaining. But he soon woke up when they reached the theatre and it was time for him to black his face and neck and hands. Cecily sat in her mother's dressing-room until it was time for the show to begin, watching her get ready and offering helpful and unhelpful criticism.

"Why not a touch of carmine on your chin, Mamma? I think it would make you look more youthful."

"My darling Cecily," said Seraphina at last in exasperation. "I have been putting on the same stage make-up ever since I was fourteen, and I know only too well that it would need more than a touch of carmine on the chin to make me look youthful."

"Oh, well, Mamma, there's no need for Portia to be such a *vewy* young girl, is there?" said Cecily, trying to be comforting.

None of the Mannerings appeared in the short curtain-raiser this evening, but they heard the tepid applause that greeted it. Barney Fidgett came off shaking his white head.

"It's bad – bad – " he said, "only about twelve in the pit, one box and a very noisy gallery."

"May I go through the pass-door, Papa," asked Cecily, "to get into the theatre?"

"Yes, my dear. The manager will show you to a box. I should take the stage level one."

Cecily sailed out without her hat now, and with an Indian shawl thrown across her shoulders over her beautiful new gown. It was mauve with a very tiny waist and voluminous skirts. As soon as Lexy walked on for the first time she saw how lovely Cecily looked sitting in the box. She was sitting well forward, with one hand under her chin, and her profile turned to the rest of the audience. There

were very few people in the pit, and half of them were watching Cecily and not the show. The only other box occupied was the one directly opposite Cecily's on a level with the stage. There was a young man seated in it, whose opera-glasses were trained on Cecily, and never once turned towards the stage. Cecily appeared to be completely unconscious of this, and seemed absorbed in what was happening on the stage. Occasionally, at anything touching, she would sigh and her long lashes would flutter with emotion.

"What a pity she can't act like that on the stage," thought Lexy and then saw that her father's eye was on her because she was swaying slightly, for her legs ached. She hastily pulled herself together and concentrated on being a page at Portia's court.

In the interval, Cecily came round and tidied her hair in her mother's mirror and they waited in vain for her to make some comment upon the show – whether or not she liked their performances – but she could not talk of anything but how dowdy the audience looked. Then, yawning at the prospect of two more hours of Shakespeare, she returned to her box. During the next part of the show she did not seem to be quite so wide-eyed in her study of the stage and sometimes Lexy could have sworn that she seemed to be looking more across at the other side of the theatre than at the actors. She did not come round in the next interval and, lo and behold, when the curtain went up again, her box was empty. And so was the one on the other side of the stage. All through the trial scene, Seraphina and Joshua were casting worried glances at the empty box. During the change of set before the last scene, while Seraphina was changing out of her lawyer's robes into the beautiful green and gold brocade gown she wore for the last scene, there was a hurried discussion between her and Joshua.

"Well, if she's not there, pray where is she?"

"Oh dear," wailed Seraphina. "Perhaps she has been stolen away by robbers – to hold her up for ransom. She was very conspicuous sitting there. We should not have let her take a box alone, Joshua. It was not proper. We should have asked the manager to sit with her."

"I'll go out front and search for her," Joshua rose imperiously, still wearing Shylock costume.

"Not in a false nose, my love!" cried Seraphina, shocked.

"Well, then, send Lexy. She can be spared from the next scene." He strode to the door. "Lexy!"

Lexy was helping the scene-shifters in the quick change but she came running up in her scarlet page's costume.

"Listen, me child. Put on your cloak, rub off your make-up and run through to the front of the house and see if you can see your sister. She is no longer in the box, and your mother fears for her safety."

"But what about the last scene?"

"You need not appear. Off you go."

Lexy wiped her face on a make-up towel, and sped off, creeping silently through the pass-door, as the curtain went up on Lorenzo and Jessica. There was no sign of Cecily in the box, nor in the pit nor at the back of the theatre. Lexy walked out into the foyer, which was deserted but for the manager who leaned against a pillar, gloomily thinking about the night's takings.

"I beg your pardon, sir," said Lexy shyly, "but have you seen my sister?"

"What's that? What's that?"

"My sister, sir. She was in a box and now she – she's not in the box."

The manager smiled rather slyly. "Ah, so the lady in the box is another Miss Mannering, is she, Miss Mannering?"

"Yes, sir."

"Then you'll find her in the refreshment-room, if you must. But I somehow think that she'll not be needing her little sister at the present time." He smirked and turned away. Lexy hurried into the refreshment-room, and her mouth fell open. There, sitting at a little table, sipping something out of a wine-glass, was Cecily with the young gentleman who had been in the opposite box. They were laughing and chattering as though they had known each other a lifetime. Lexy stood like a small statue in the doorway. Then Cecily caught sight of her:

"Well, I declare – here's little Lexy. Just fancy, Alexandwa, who should have taken the opposite box but Mr Horton whom I met last vacation at the Honouwable Poppy Pagett's. It *is* a small world, now isn't it?"

"Is this a sister of yours, Miss Mannering?" asked the gentleman in surprise, looking at Lexy's straight hair and prominent teeth and her shabby old cloak with red tights and shoes with turned-up toes appearing beneath it.

"Yes, indeed. Do you not see the family likeness?"

"Er – charming – charming," said the young man, embarrassed. Lexy thought him very handsome, and dressed in the height of fashion with peg-top trousers, and very fine whiskers.

"Mamma and Papa were worried, Cecily," she said. "They thought you were being taken by robbers and held for ransom."

"And so she is, Miss Alexandra," the young man said laughing. "And she knows what the ransom is. But as our terms are already arranged, I will return her to her loving parents for a while." Cecily blushed prettily and rose, sweeping her skirts.

"I declare, Mr Horton, you talk more nonsense than any gentleman I ever met. Wansom, indeed! Lexy – you may tell Mamma and Papa that I was having a glass of clawet cup with an old fwiend."

Lexy shook her head. "No, I can't say that. They'd be vexed."

"But it is particularly *weak* claret cup in this refreshment bar," obsered Mr Horton.

"It's not that, sir. It's because she didn't stay to see the last act they will be vexed. You see, she ought to be following the part of Nerissa, because she'll be playing it soon."

"Will she? H'm," he looked at Cecily thoughtfully. "Then perhaps we should return to our separate loges," he said.

He kissed Cecily's hand gallantly. "Farewell – from a grateful robber." Then he turned to Lexy. "And goodbye, little sister. I think you take your part excellently. Remember me, won't you?"

"Yes, sir."

Under the curious eyes of the refreshment server, they made their way back into the theatre. Cecily waved to Mr Horton as they parted, each to go down a little corridor on either side of the foyer that led to the boxes. Lexy accompanied Cecily and whispered, "I shall not say that you met Mr Horton."

"As you wish," Cecily shrugged her shoulders and closed the door of the box.

When she got back-stage, Lexy found that there was an atmosphere of strain. The gallery was getting restive. As long as the character of Shylock had dominated the play they had been interested. They had booed and hissed and cat-called every time he had entered, and then in the trial scene had cheered loudly at his defeat. But now that he was obviously out of the story for good, their interest was warning. The tying up of the ends of the story did not seem to interest them at all and they talked and fought and spat orange pips over the balcony down into the mercifully empty pit. The players on the stage could hardly make themselves heard. Seraphina was getting more upset and Joshua stood on the side of the stage making gestures of turning a handle, in an effort to make the actors speed up and finish the play as quickly as possible, before the gallery got completely out of hand. Then suddenly the unexpected happened. From the box opposite Cecily a figure leaned out and shook a fist threateningly up at the "gods".

"Quiet up there, you ruffians," he shouted, "or shall I come up and quieten you myself?"

" 'Ark at the swell!" jeered one voice, but there was comparative quiet afterwards. And the play was finished as quickly as possible. At the curtain call, the gallery applauded generously and called for Shylock, but there was not a sign of life from the pit. Joshua stepped forward, bowed low to the two boxes and then spoke to the gallery.

"Thank you, my friends, for understanding the quality of mercy," he said wryly, and they screamed with delight.

"Nothing but wild animals," murmured Joshua, as the curtain descended, "beasts of the field – "

"Audiences – pah – " fumed old Matthew Tollerton, "I've always hated 'em."

Joshua and Seraphina found Lexy in the wings: "And where was your sister?" they demanded.

"She went to the ladies' retiring-room," said Lexy, thinking that as Cecily had probably done so during the evening it wasn't really a lie.

"She was gone a long time," observed Joshua.

"She should have come back-stage," said Seraphina crossly, "and not worried us so."

Cecily came running into her parents' dressing-room

and kissed them both: "Oh, Mamma – how sweetly pwetty you looked, and Papa, I so enjoyed your Shylock. And that was all the gallewy cared for, wasn't it? And fancy that gentleman speaking to them like that."

"Yes, it was a noble gesture," agreed Joshua. "I should have liked to thank him for it."

Cecily very slowly closed one eye at Lexy who hastily covered her face with her make-up towel. It was nice to have a secret with Cecily, even though it was not quite the same sort as the mouse in Mr Tollerton's boots.

"What a night," sighed Seraphina on the way home. "I felt so sorry for the audience – what there was of them. I loved them so. I felt that if only I could have done a really cheery number with some comedy dancing I could have held them."

"Hush, me dear," said Joshua, "your days of cheery numbers are over. You must remember that you are a classical actress now."

"Well, *I* enjoyed it," said Cecily, who was walking lightly along with her head in the air. "It was the best evening I have spent for – oh, such a long time."

"Better than when you were at the Misses Dingwaters'?" asked her father quizzically.

"Oh, much, much better, Papa," said Cecily.

A rather sleepy landlord was waiting up for them at the lodgings. He said gloomily: "Don't suppose you 'ad much of a 'ouse."

"Your supposition is only too correct," said Joshua.

"Nay, they don't care for Shakespeare in Oldcastle," said the landlord, and brought in the pease-pudding and cold ham that was for supper.

As Lexy and Cecily lay in bed, Cecily said in a funny tone of voice, "What did you think of Mr Horton?"

"I thought him very handsome," said Lexy, "and brave too, to shout out to the gallery like that."

"Yes," said Cecily, "Handsome and bwave – and wich too!"

"Is he an honourable?" Lexy enquired.

"No, Lexy. His father is Sir Bartlett Horton, but he is only a knight, so I should not have a title. Sir Bartlett is a mill-owner."

"*You* – have a title? What do you mean?"

"Go to sleep, Lexy."

And Lexy was soon too sleepy to puzzle her head further on the subject.

CHAPTER 3

Burlesque

By the following Wednesday it was quite clear that they did not care for Shakespeare in Oldcastle.

"Very well, then," said Joshua, "they shall not have it." And they put on a melodrama in modern dress, which Joshua considered trashy, but which was one of Seraphina's favourites. This was the one in which Clem played little Sir Randolph, wearing a blue velvet suit that he and the audience adored. It made Lexy feel sick to look at him being so cloyingly angelic on the stage. She wished she could go out front and tell the audience that his last action before going on was to paint the baby's face with greasepaint, giving him a bright red nose!

But even this pandering to the popular taste did not bring in the public. The takings were still as poor as ever. The more gloomy the theatre manager became, the more optimistic was Joshua.

"We'll advertise outside the theatre the return of Miss Cecily Mannering after six years' retirement – and we'll put in the new burlesque on Friday. Friday is pay-day, so they should come in then, if ever. And a new Mannering is sure to be an attraction."

47

"But the burlesque is hardly ready, my love," said Seraphina. "Cecily doesn't seem to know her lines."

"She soon will, when she hears that it's to go on on Friday."

But Cecily merely yawned and said, "I suppose I should make up my mind what I am to wear," and spent the whole evening sewing on flounces.

At supper on the Thursday, Joshua said, "I am afraid that no salaries can be paid until after tomorrow night's show." This was quite a usual happening and no one was surprised. The bills went up outside advertising the return of Miss Cecily Mannering in a new burlesque, but caused no particular interest.

"It *must* bring them in," seethed Joshua, "otherwise we shan't be able to pay the salaries, and that has never happened in one of my companies before."

Everyone else was very nervous on Cecily's behalf but she didn't seem to mind at all.

"Oh, well, if I dwy, I dwy," she said carelessly.

"And what of the other people on the stage with you?" asked Lexy.

"Let them get out of it as best they can. I shall just feel like laughing."

This sounded like blasphemy to Lexy's ears. "They'll be vexed," she warned Cecily, "especially Mr Tollerton."

"Mr Tollerton is always vexed," laughed Cecily, "so what diffewence will it make?"

On Friday night the audience was just as small as ever. Joshua peered through a chink in the curtain and groaned.

"We'll never get out," he said, meaning that they would never clear their expenses for the week.

Cecily, looking ravishing in one of her new gowns, was joking on the stage with Courtney Stanton before the curtain went up. There was a spatter of applause at her entrance, which soon died down when she started to speak. Joshua was leaning up against a piece of scenery in the wings with one arm raised over his eyes in despair as Cecily mumbled and fluffed and dried through her part. Once she was given a prompt which she could not hear and said quite loudly, "I beg your pardon?"

"I cannot believe she is my daughter," groaned Joshua.

Matthew Tollerton became more and more furious as the play progressed and rattled off his lines at a great rate, which was always a sign of his annoyance. There was not a laugh at all during the first ten minutes – then suddenly Cecily forgot her lines altogether and said the closing lines of the play and the curtain came down.

Joshua came storming on to the stage. "Who dared to bring down that curtain?" he roared.

"Miss Mannering spoke the curtain line, sir," said the prompter nervously.

"Then she should have been prompted until she got the right line and finished the play."

"I'm sowwy, Papa, but I went wrong and well – that was the only line I could think of."

"But do you realise you've cut twenty minutes out of the bill? The audience will complain – why, we shan't run three hours!"

"And quite long enough – to such an audience as this, Papa," said Cecily carelessly. "Fwankly, I should advise you to tell them that the next piece has a happy ending and advise them all to go home."

"Me girl, you are a fool!" said Joshua quietly.

Lexy felt that she would have died if her father had spoken to her like that, but Cecily just laughed and said to Lexy:

"You should have seen Mr Tollerton's face when I said the tag line!"

After the melodrama was over, the manager came round with a face longer than ever.

"Mr Mannering," he said, "a dozen or so of the audience asked for their money back, because the bill was so short. I had to give it to them."

"Confound them!" cried Joshua. "Now we most certainly shan't get out."

The company were lurking in the corridor outside Joshua's dressing-room, hoping to be paid. Stern-faced, Joshua sat at his dressing-table counting out money into separate piles. Then the company came in one by one and received their money. Instantly their spirits soared and off they hurried to the pie-shop or "The Black Bull". Then Joshua turned to the family. His face was white and set.

"We have lost heavily this week," he said. "There are no salaries for us. And what is more, when I have paid for the transportation of the theatre baggage, there will not be enough to pay our railway fares to Marlingford on Sunday. I have enough for the rest of the company – but not for us, and what we make on the two houses tomorrow will have to pay the baggage."

"Does that mean – walking?" asked Seraphina heavily.

Once before after a bad week, they had had to walk to the next town, but that had not been far.

"Marlingford is thirty miles away," said Joshua, "I

50

could do it between Saturday and Monday, but you could not, my precious, and neither could Clem.''

"Nor could I,'' joined in Cecily hastily.

"I'll walk with you, Papa,'' said Lexy eagerly, "if you can find means to send the others.''

"No, no, it's too far,'' said Seraphina. "You would not be fit for a performance when you arrived.''

But Lexy persisted that she was willing, for there was nothing that she loved better than long walks with her father. It was the only chance that she got of seeing the countryside, and as they walked through the lanes, Joshua would declaim from Shakespeare at the top of his splendid voice. It sounded even better out in the country air than it did confined in a theatre, she thought. They would stop at some inn for bread and cheese and mulled cyder, and when they arrived at their lodgings Lexy always felt as though she had had a holiday.

"No, we must find the money for the fares somehow,'' said Joshua. "I dare not borrow from the company. They would lend it gladly I know, but it would never do for the artistes to guess that the management was penniless. It would take away their confidence and they would seek other engagements.''

"Perhaps – the landlord of our lodgings,'' suggested Cecily.

"No, they are not flourishing themselves,'' said Joshua, "with the good lady ill and attended by the doctor.''

"I know, Papa,'' suggested Clem, "I'll sing on the street. I would make everyone cry.'' He was very proud of his ability to reduce audiences to tears. Seraphina kissed him on top of his head.

"Oh, my love,'' she cried, "over my dead body – ''

"Yes, that would be splendid," said Clem. "You lie in the street and pretend to be dead, and I'll sing hymns over you – and say to everyone. 'My poor Mamma is dead. Oh whatever shall I do?' and then they'll put money in my collecting box. Sovereigns, I expect."

They all laughed at this, and felt better.

"Well, we'll leave it to Providence," said Joshua. "Perhaps we shall have a better house tomorrow. After all it *is* Saturday, and the baggage expenses may be more than covered. So hie to high fortune."

"And hie home to supper," added Seraphina.

"Papa," said Lexy in a small voice. "You've forgotten something."

"What's that, my love?"

"The bill for the lodgings."

A gloom settled over them again.

"Why, yes, I had not thought of that consideration. H'm – well, God will provide. Perhaps tomorrow will be a splendid day – "

Lexy walked home troubled by the thought that God might not provide. Granted He had always done so before on similar occasions, but it seemed a bit lazy always to leave it to Him and expect Him to come to the rescue.

As they lay in bed that night she said to Cecily:

"I wish we could do something – I've not even got anything worth selling. My best dress is so threadbare that it's hardly 'best' any more. And Mamma must keep all her jewellery to wear on the stage. In any case it's all glass and tinsel."

"What a little old lady you are," said Cecily, quite affectionately. "You have the weight of the world on your shoulders, haven't you?"

Lexy sighed: "*Someone* must. Papa just says, 'God will provide'."

"Oh, well, so He will. You'll see."

Joshua had called another rehearsal of the burlesque the following morning, to make sure that the same thing did not happen as on the previous night At ten o'clock everyone was assembled on the stage, except for Cecily.

"I daren't think where the child has gone," wailed Seraphina. "She came down to the theatre with us. I do wish she would not keep disappearing in such an alarming way."

Joshua fumed round the stage: "I can't dismiss my own daughter, otherwise I would. Break for a quarter of an hour, ladies and gentlemen. And my apologies on behalf of my daughter."

Lexy was very glad of the opportunity to pop over to the pie-shop and have a glass of hot cordial with the last half-penny of her previous week's pocket-money. All the company were murmuring about Cecily's unpunctuality, as well as her lack of talent, poor memory for lines and general uselessness.

"But ladylike – " Courtney Stanton kept on putting in. "She's the essence of a lady."

They returned to the theatre and dispersed to do odd jobs in their dressing-rooms. At some time past eleven Cecily sailed into the theatre, looking flushed and happy and shouted out: "Papa, Papa dear – have you been waiting for me?"

"The effrontery of it," fumed Matthew Tollerton. "I'd like to see that happen in any theatre in my young days – daughter or no daughter!"

Joshua said nothing but gave orders to run through

the burlesque. He sat in the pit and when it was finished he said, "Again please." When it was over once more he dismissed the other members of the cast and ordered Lexy to read their lines while Cecily went over her part again and again.

"But Papa," complained Cecily, "it's getting vewy late and I shall have no time for luncheon, if we are to wehearse again this afternoon."

"And neither shall I," said Joshua implacably. "Lexy, you may go. I do not see why you should suffer for your sister's idiocies."

"No, I'll stay," said Lexy.

"Oh, Joshua," pleaded Seraphina, "let the poor lambs have a bite to eat. They'll come over faint during the afternoon."

"If Cecily can go through the whole piece once more, there will be just time to buy herself a pie, before we recommence," said Joshua.

Cecily's hunger must have stimulated her memory, for she managed to get through it with only an occasional "Oh, no, that's wrong" and "Oh, let me see – yes, I know."

The first house was very sparse with a lot of babes-in-arms who all cried loudly during the quiet parts of the show. The audience ate sweetmeats and rustled the paper, and sucked oranges audibly.

"Why cannot they stay at home and guzzle in their own parlours?" demanded Matthew Tollerton at the end of the burlesque, when the audience did not even bother to applaud.

Lexy enjoyed the break between the first and second houses on a Saturday. The whole company always took tea together, usually in the wardrobe. Gertrude Tollerton supervised the wardrobe, as well as playing the heavier character parts and she would make the tea, and bring in cakes and buns, and then they all sat round on the big wicker skips, still in their make-up and costumes and they all ate and drank and the men told stories of their theatrical experiences, while the kindly Mrs Tollerton presided over the tea-urn. Today Joshua was absent. He was poring over the accounts with the theatre manager. And so the atmosphere was inclined to be that of a school when the headmaster is not present. Barney Fidgett rode Clem round the room on his shoulders, and Cecily and Courtney giggled and whispered in a corner.

"Has Papa found any way for us to travel to Marlingford?" Lexy whispered to Seraphina.

"I cannot say, my precious. But he is with the manager now so perhaps some way will be found. Don't worry your little head."

Lexy sat rocking Jamie on her knee, and feeling pleasantly drowsy in the warmth and comfort. It was quite a wrench to go down and get ready for the second house, at which they were doing "The Clown's Revenge" and "A Midsummer-Night's Dream", as this was considered a nice light Saturday-evening bill. Lexy played Mustardseed and Clem played Puck. Cecily was playing the Singing Fairy, although her voice was rather thin and did not carry. But she looked so divine that no-one really cared. As soon as Lexy went on she saw that Cecily's Mr Horton was in a box again. He smiled at her broadly as she came on and while Cecily was singing, "You spotted snakes with double tongue," he sat with his opera-glasses focused on her, and clapped and shouted "encore" at the end of it.

The audience, although small, seemed to be more

appreciative than they had been the whole week. The flying on wires impressed them considerably as it had never been seen in Oldcastle before, and every time Clem or the fairy flew in, they were greeted with applause.

Although the harness hurt her rather under the arms, Lexy liked the flying: it was so much like the dreams that she sometimes had of floating effortlessly up and down stairs.

When they took the curtain call there was a lovely bouquet handed up for Cecily, with a card in an envelope attached. She read it, then crumpled it up hastily when the curtain fell.

"An admirer!" cried Seraphina. "Why, Cecily, you are a sly puss."

In the bustle of the strike, when all the scenery was taken down and loaded into the cart that would take it to the station, and the costumes were folded up in the skips, Cecily seemed to disappear. Saturday night was always a very late night, as Joshua did not care to leave the theatre until everything was cleared up, and his family did not relish walking home alone through the strange dark streets. It was on Saturday nights that Lexy most often envied Jamie in his comfortable basket.

It was late when Joshua, looking weary and distraught, at last sank down in a chair in his dressing-room. Clem was asleep sitting in another chair, and Lexy was rocking Jamie's basket. Seraphina was finishing packing up her make-up.

"I wonder where Cecily has got to again. Really she does disappear in the strangest way," said Seraphina.

Just then Cecily came into the room, wearing her wrap, with her face flushed, and eyes shining.

"Where have you been?" demanded Joshua.

"Taking some air at the stage-door, Papa."

"Well, Joshua," said Seraphina, "what is to become of us tomorrow?"

Joshua sighed and passed his hand over his eyes wearily. "I have settled the baggage and the lodgings. There is now not a farthing left.'"

"Then what are we to do?" cried Seraphina. "How are we to get to Marlingford?"

Clem woke up and started to grizzle.

"I don't want to walk, Mamma," he wailed. "I don't want to walk."

"You shan't, my pet, you shan't," Seraphina comforted him. "Oh, Joshua, what are we to do?"

"Don't fwet, Mamma," said Cecily, crossing to her mother and putting her arm round her shoulders. "See, we have been provided for." And from her pocket she produced a handful of sovereigns. The rest of the family gaped.

"Cecily," gasped Lexy, "you didn't borrow from – "

But Cecily cut her short.

"No, I didn't bowwow. I've been to the pawnbwokers for the first time in my life. Oh, it was most intewesting. I'd only got a few little things – You know, the locket that the Honouwable Poppy Pagett gave me last Chwistmas and a cameo bwooch that her bwother gave me at the same time. And then there were a few little twinkets given to me by others of the girls at school. Their value was gweater than I hoped. See, Papa, is this enough for us to get to Marlingford?"

Joshua counted it eagerly: "Enough for all," he said.

"But, my love," said Seraphina, kissing Cecily, "why should you sell your few trinkets for us?"

"There were only twashy little things," said Cecily carelessly. "One day I shall have weal jewels."

"You shall be repaid, me child, as soon as Fortune favours us," said Joshua, "that I promise you. And then you may reclaim your trinkets."

"I shall not bother," said Cecily. "After all, they're not large enough to show up on the stage."

Joshua kissed her on the top of her head. He was deeply affected.

"Me child, those are the most gallant words I have heard you say. I am proud of you, my daughter – was that where you had gone this morning when you were absent?"

"Yes, Papa."

"Then I apologise for my anger," Joshua bowed, then added: "But don't let it happen again."

Cecily laughed: "Oh, Papa, you are funny! But I'm not *too* bad a girl, am I?"

"You're wonderful, Cecily," said Lexy.

"Absolutely prime," said Clem, and went to sleep again.

CHAPTER 4

No Place for a Baby

On Monday night, the opening night of their week at Marlingford, there was a crisis. The baggage had not arrived. That meant no costumes, no properties, no scenery! And the bill was to be "The Truth about Harlequin" and "King Lear". Joshua was nearly tearing his hair.

"Very well, we must do 'The Clown's Revenge' and one of the modern pieces," he said, "and everyone can wear their day clothes. I'll beg, borrow or steal some furniture."

Somehow they collected enough pieces of furniture to set the bare stage, with just curtains as scenery. And then, half an hour before the curtain was to go up, the baggage arrived. There was an immediate chaos of unpacking, scene-shifting and dressing.

"We'll do the original bill," announced Joshua, pulling out his robes for King Lear from a skip. In their dressing-room Joshua and Seraphina had to dress and make-up at top speed.

"Oh, dear," sighed Seraphina, "I need an hour at least to look like Cordelia." She swept a lot of rubbish off her dressing place with a hurried gesture and in doing so she knocked Jamie's basket. It woke him and he started to cry.

"Oh, no!" groaned Seraphina. "If he starts that I cannot stand it."

For, although Jamie was usually a good baby, once he started to cry there was no stopping him. This was obviously going to be one of his bad evenings.

Cecily came in from the dressing-room next door.

"Mamma," she said. "Jamie's cwying."

"Yes," said Seraphina patiently, "I hear him."

"Well, what is the matter with him? Is there a pin sticking into him?"

"He is just crying," said Seraphina. "Babies do."

Cecily rocked his basket rather gingerly. "Poor wee man," she crooned, "had he got a pin, then?" But Jamie only cried louder.

"Leave him alone," ordered Joshua, "and finish your toilet."

"I hardly know what costume to put on," said Cecily maddeningly. "First we're to do this, and then that, and then this again. It's weally most diswacting."

"We are returning to the original bill," said Joshua. "You are a noblewoman of the court, if you remember. As soon as you can get Cordelia into that flibbertigibbet brain of yours, you shall play Cordelia and your mother Goneril."

"Oh, I shan't know Cordelia for months, Papa," said Cecily airily, "and she's such a dull cweature."

Joshua opened his mouth to pour out his views on the subject and then closed it again. Jamie increased the volume of his yelling.

"Weally, mamma," said Cecily, "a dwessing-woom is no place for a baby. You can't expect the poor mite to

60

sleep in all the noise. And it's so unhealthy, too – dusty and dirty, and the gas-light on all the time. Why don't you leave him in the lodgings?"

"What? All alone? Never! You'd not get a landlady who would stay in every evening to look after him."

"I'm sure you would this week. Old Mother Bason doesn't go gadding out of an evening, Mamma. She's far too old."

"I would not care to leave little Jamie with that black and midnight hag," said Joshua. "Why, she smokes cheroots. She'd drop ash all over him."

"It's a bad enough habit in a man," agreed Seraphina. "In a woman, it is revolting."

"But she need not actually *sit* with Jamie. She could wemain in her own basement. As long as there is someone in the house, he would be quite safe."

"But what if he woke and cried?"

"Then she would hear him and comfort him."

"I wouldn't like to be comforted by Mrs Bason," said Lexy, who had just come into the room. "It would frighten me."

"You be quiet, Lexy," said Cecily. "It's for Jamie's good. It's not safe for him in here, with evewyone changing and wampaging about. He'll get knocked off the dwessing-table."

Jamie bellowed louder, as though in horror at the thought.

"The stage-manager asked me to call overture and beginners," Lexy got in at last.

"Well, why did you not say so?" roared Joshua, rising from his chair.

"But Joshua, what are we to do about Jamie?" demanded Seraphina.

"Oh, let him cry," said Joshua angrily, "and tomorrow leave him with Mother Bason."

Cecily was delighted at having won her point.

"I'm sure he'll be happier, the poor mite, than being cawwied backwards and forwards, in his basket evewy evening."

Jamie screamed forlornly and held up his little pink hands as if in despair. Lexy picked him up and rocked him for a little while, frowning at the thought of leaving him to the tender mercies of Mrs Bason. But then she remembered that she had promised the prompter to "hold the book" for him during the burlesque, so that he could hurry out for a bite of something which he had not been able to do previously because of the muddle over the baggage, so she had to put Jamie down and hurry out.

Next day at breakfast, Seraphina said to Mrs Bason, "Will you be at home this evening, Mrs Bason?"

"Ay – " said Mrs Bason, non-committally.

"I wonder if you would be so good as to keep an eye on Baby if we leave him up in our room?"

"Ay – " said Mrs Bason, dropping ash from her cheroot very near the bowl of porridge she was just handing to Joshua. Joshua shuddered and said, "We shall, of course, reimburse you for this small service."

"Ay – " was the only comment.

"Do you think she heard?" whispered Seraphina to Cecily, as Mrs Bason disappeared into the scullery.

Mrs Bason certainly did resemble one of the witches from "Macbeth". She was a widow, and in her flowing widow's weeds, with lank grey hair and the eternal cheroot hanging on her lower lip, one expected her to burst into "Double, double, toil and trouble" at any moment. When she bent to stir the porridge saucepan, the likeness was so vivid that Lexy giggled nervously.

"Well, shall we leave him during the day-time too?" asked Seraphina.

"No," objected Joshua. "He must have *some* fresh air."

"I don't think the air of this town in any fwesher than at Oldcastle," complained Cecily fastidiously.

Marlingford had been a small market town, but now there were steel works springing up in and around it and the factories and workshops were spoiling the quiet beauty of the old town. As they walked to the theatre, they recognised landmarks that were fast being swallowed up in a grey tide of industry.

"Oh, dear," sighed Cecily. "How I wish I had not to wehearse all day. I should so love to look at the shops."

"Look at the shops!" grunted Joshua. "You've got enough long rôles to learn to keep you busy for a month of Sundays. Now mind you watch your mother rehearsing this afternoon, and follow her lines."

"Yes," sighed Cecily, casting longing glances at a haberdasher's shop that they passed which displayed an enticing array of caps and ribbons.

"I think we shall have a good week here. Last night was excellent for a Monday," announced Joshua optimistically. "It should restore our fortunes. Marlingford is not yet so industrial as Oldcastle. There are still some gentry who will, I hope, come in for the theatre nearer the end of the week."

"Weally, Papa?" said Cecily warmly. "Oh, it will be much pleasanter than playing to mill-workers and the like."

"One mill-worker with a taste for Shakespeare is worth as much as one squire, me girl. Remember that."

"Why no, Papa," argued Cecily. "The mill-worker would sit in the gallewy; the squire might take a box."

"I was not speaking of money, my child."

"Your papa has such high ideals," said Seraphina fondly.

Lexy could see Cecily opening her mouth to say, "But ideals don't pay wailway fares," so she hastily said very loudly, "Oh, Cecily, look at that lady's curious bonnet. Do you care for it?"

At the theatre, the company were jubilant. They were being made so welcome in the town and a reporter on a local paper had already been round to interview them.

"It *will* be a good week," cried Seraphina. "Oh, I feel it in my bones. And you shall get your jewellery back, my precious, from the person to whom you lent it," she whispered to Cecily.

The whole atmosphere at the theatre was gayer than at Oldcastle. The green-room seemed to be a social centre of the town, and during the morning rehearsal the manager was bringing some of the local gentry in to meet the players who were not actually on the stage. The walls of the green-room were covered with pictures of famous actors who had played there – Macready, the two Keans, Mrs Siddons and a host of not-so-famous ones who were well-known to the Mannerings. Their lunch was brought into the green-room, and took longer than usual as there were visitors present.

"Run and brush your hair, Lexy," Seraphina had whispered as soon as she had seen that there were strangers about. Cecily had brought out her best Indian shawl without being told, and was charming an elderly gentleman who still wore the old-fashioned knee breeches and buckled shoes of his youth.

The night's bill consisted of "The Clown's Revenge" and "Julius Caesar". Julius Caesar was one of Joshua's best parts. Lexy always thought that he looked at his most noble wearing a laurel wreath. It was one of the lightest plays for the women, for Seraphina played Portia, Mrs Tollerton Calpurnia. Clem and Lexy played servants and Cecily was a citizeness for this production. They always had to have "supers" to take the parts of soldiers and this afternoon Joshua was drilling them on the stage. As usual they were a poor-looking lot, the scum of the town, who did casual work as labourers, crossing-sweepers, and anything that was going. Seraphina always maintained that they were the best parts of "Julius Caesar" because they always made the audience laugh so. But Joshua had no patience with them and would roar and rant at them for hours on end in an effort to gain some effect.

When they went back to the lodgings at tea-time, Serpahina said to Mrs Bason, "You'll not forget that the baby is upstairs, will you?"

"Nay," said Mrs Bason, by way of a change.

They left Jamie sleeping peacefully in his basket in his parents' room, after they had all kissed him goodnight, as though they were leaving him for weeks. Half-way down the stairs, Seraphina stopped: "No, Joshua, I can't leave the mite behind like this."

Joshua drew her down the stairs by her hand.

"Nonsense, my precious. He will have the best sleep he's had for many weeks and you are not to fret after him."

The theatre was full for the evening's performance, and there were even a few enthusiastic admirers at the stage-door. Joshua's manner became more cheerful and genial than it had been for weeks. He called his fellow actors "me lad" and "old boy" and his family "me loves". Seraphina's eyes began to get their old shine back again.

"This is more how it generally is," Lexy told Cecily. "Not like Oldcastle. You joined us at a bad week, you know."

The burlesque that Cecily was in went better than it had done before. She only dried three times and the audience laughed at all the nonsense in it. The change of set from the burlesque to "Julius Caesar" was a heavy one and Lexy was running around in her short little page's tunic, helping the stage-manager and the scene-shifters. The space at the back of the stage was rather limited, and so some pieces of furniture had to be put just outside the door that led to an open courtyard. Lexy was carrying a small table out there when suddenly she noticed a red glow in the sky.

"What's that?" she demanded of one of the supers, who was having a quiet smoke outside.

"Furnace, I don't doubt." Then he looked again. "Nay, it's fire," he exclaimed. "Quite near, by the looks on it."

Together they ran out into the street.

"Where's fire?" he demanded of a passer-by.

"Oop Marlegate," was the answer.

Lexy's heart turned over. Marlegate. That was where their lodgings were. Without another thought she turned and started to run, still in her brief tunic. People turned and stared at the quaint little figure as she streaked along, panting and breathless, in tights and Roman sandals. She was positive that it was their lodgings that were on fire.

"Supposing it isn't, though," she thought, "and I'm late back for the rest of the show. Papa will think I've lost my senses, running off to look at fires! But then, supposing it is!"

She quickened her pace. The last part was uphill and her heart felt as though it would burst. At last she turned a corner and could see where the flames were coming from. Yes, it *was* their lodgings! The house next to it was flaming as well. Half of the building had caught but it was not the half in which the staircase was situated nor the room in which lay Jamie in his basket. Perhaps Mrs Bason had already removed him. There was a crowd of people gaping up at the houses, but no sign of a fire brigade or of any effort being made to check the fire. Lexy turned to one of the onlookers.

"Where's Mrs Bason?" she demanded.

"Oo?" came the question.

"The lady from that house."

"Ee – Mrs Bason, you mean. She's yonder – took poorly, poor body."

Lexy pushed her way through the cluster of people. Lying on her back on a blanket was Mrs Bason, moaning painfully, having something poured through her lips from a flask.

"Where's Jamie?" shouted Lexy loudly above the chatter of the crowd and the crackling of the fire. No one took the slightest notice of her. She looked up at the flames. They were spreading more to the other side of the house. Suddenly she ran across the street and in through the open front door. A wall of smoke came up and hit her so that she coughed and reeled. She had to make her way up the staircase almost by touch. Already the flames were beginning to lick across the hallway towards the bannisters. Up two flights she went and opened the door of the room where Jamie was. He lay in his basket, kicking and crowing with joy at the pretty pink light that was coming in through the window. Lexy picked him up in his basket and looked quickly round the room. What was to become of all their belongings? But she could carry no more – and the staircase might have caught fire already. She ran to the door and looked down. The whole of the bannisters were on fire, making a wall of flame down one side of the staircase. The heat was intense. Lexy pulled up the covers over Jamie's face, and plunged down the stairs. She thought that at any minute the leaping tongues of flames would catch her hair. But at last she reached the front door, only to find that it had slammed to behind her. She had to put Jamie down on the scorchingly hot floor-boards while she wrestled to get the door open. The metal latch was so hot that it burned her fingers.

At last they were out in the fresh air, in the blessedly cool fresh air. Lexy filled her lungs with it, and swayed slightly. The crowd began to advance on her, crying, "Look, it's a baby in the basket," and "Oh, the little mite," and she felt that she could not stand this. Then she remembered the time. She must have been a quarter of an hour at least. She picked Jamie out of the basket and held him in the crook of one arm; she took his basket in the other hand and turned and ran down the hill. The crowd shouted after her, but she did not wait. There was a crash as the roof of the neighbouring house gave way and burning pieces of cinder and ash floated down the road. She ran to the theatre

almost as quickly as she had come. Fire or no fire she must not be late for her entrance. She ran into her father's and mother's empty dressing-room, deposited Jamie, and hurried on to the stage just in time, as the curtain rose. She was glad that she had no lines to say, for she was almost choking for breath and tried to keep as closely behind other people as possible to hide the state she was in.

It was a crowd scene, and Cecily, passing her, hissed in her ear, "You look disgwaceful, child. What have you been doing?"

"Wait till I tell!" whispered Lexy.

When she had a few minutes to spare she ran to her dressing-room and looked in the glass. She did look terrible. She had great black smears all across her face, and her hair was all ruffled and singed at the ends. No wonder her mother and father had been looking at her rather hard. She heard her mother moving about in the next room, and went in there. Seraphina did not seem to have noticed Jamie.

"Lexy," she exclaimed, "you looked like a street-child on the stage. Have you been romping out in that yard with the supers? It's not ladylike, I tell you."

Lexy did not say anything. She just looked at her mother, not knowing where to begin. Perhaps it would be as well not to tell her until after the play was over.

"I'm sorry, Mamma," said Lexy and went out of the room.

It was not until they were packing up to go home that Seraphina noticed her son. Then she clapped a hand over her mouth to stifle a scream.

"Joshua," she said in a terrified whisper, "am I suffering from hallucinations?"

"What's that, me dear?"

"Look, look – there's Jamie. We left him at home – I'm going out of my senses – " She advanced slowly and touched him as though to see if he were real. Jamie clutched at her finger, smiling recognition.

"Oh, my lamb – just look at him. All smuts and dirt – just as Lexy was – Joshua, what can have happened?"

Joshua came and looked at him. "It's Jamie, right enough," he said at length.

"Of course it's Jamie – but how did he get here?"

"Call for Lexy."

As soon as Lexy came into the room she said, "Mamma, now don't be upset. But our lodgings caught fire. I saw the red in the sky and felt sure what it was, so I ran there and brought little Jamie back."

Seraphina burst into tears. Joshua picked Lexy up and sat her on his knee.

"My brave girl," he said, "now tell us all about it."

Lexy told them about Mrs Bason, and the way the crowd had collected and done nothing.

"And the house?"

"It will be gone by now," said Lexy.

"All our possessions," said Joshua dully.

"Not all," said Seraphina, crooning over Jamie.

"Well, at least, we had no savings there to be destroyed," said Joshua wryly. "Now, what have we lost? All our day clothes, and toilet things. Is that all?"

"Yes," said Seraphina. "My jewellery is here, and even a few gowns in with my costumes."

"My books – " said Joshua.

"All Cecily's lovely dresses," said Lexy.

"Yes, Cecily must be told."

When Cecily heard the news she had hysterics and

cried distractedly, "My lilac gwenadine, my new taffeta, my organdies – Oh cwuel – cwuel – " But when Seraphina told her how Lexy had rescued Jamie, she quietened down.

"But how could the fire have started?" she demanded.

"That old Mrs Bason left one of her cheroots about, I'll warrant," said Seraphina.

"I wish she had been all burnt up," said Clem ghoulishly.

The company walked up to Marlegate with them to see how bad the damage had been. The whole house had gone, and those on either side were still on fire. Poor Mrs Bason had been taken to the infirmary suffering from shock.

"Where are we to go tonight, then?" said Seraphina.

They enquired round amongst the company to see if there were any vacancies in their lodgings, but there were none. Then Barney Fidgett approached Joshua.

"A word in your ear, Guv'nor. Knowing as we do that you have lost all in this accident, please do not take it amiss that we have collected amongst ourselves to ease your loss."

He pressed a bulging purse into Joshua's hand. "Take my advice, Guv'nor, go to the best hotel in Marlingford and get a good night's rest – you and the chicks. You all need it."

Joshua was deeply moved. He walked down the hill with one army round Barney's shoulders and the other round Lexy's. At the bottom of the hill, he turned to the little group that followed him.

"Now that this accident has occurred to our private belongings, following disastrous theatrical losses, some might call us a poor family, but if I may quote, 'I am wealthy in my friends'."

CHAPTER 5

Rivals

"Lexy, wing for the maid," said Cecily grandly when they woke next morning in an enormous four-poster bed in the Red Lion Hotel, Marlingford. Lexy, half-asleep, said "Don't be silly – " and then remembered where they were. By the side of the bed hung a long wide sash that was the bell-pull. She tugged it, and then sank back upon the soft downy mattress.

"Better than Mrs Bason's," she murmured and dozed until the entry of a neat maid in a cap and apron woke her again. Cecily ordered a sumptuous breakfast to be brought up to them in their room, and then she got out of bed and began to dress her hair, glorying in the large dressing-table and the many mirrors in which she could see the back of her head or her profile, at will.

"And now I have all these miwwors I have no clothes and jewels to twy on in them," she moaned.

"You've still got your hair," Lexy pointed out.

"So I should hope." But Cecily could not be depressed for long in such comfort as this and was soon eating the enormous breakfast that the maid brought in, and dispatching her for hot water, and to see if their boots had been cleaned. Lexy was a little over-awed at the splendour of the hotel. They had only stayed at inns occasionally on their travels, and those had been very minor ones. The Red Lion, Marlingford, had been a famous coaching inn but now, although old in appearance and traditions, it was fitted with every modern luxury – gas-light, bells in all the rooms, and toilets with running water.

Soon Seraphina sailed into the room looking more beautiful than she usually managed to in the mornings.

"Mamma," said Lexy, "how have you done it? We have no sponges or anything – "

"I have sent out for some necessaries that we *must* have. Fortunately, I had a comb and so on in my reticule. Clem, of course, takes all this as an admirable excuse for not washing but I am afraid he has been thwarted."

"Oh, Mamma," said Cecily, "is it not heaven to be in civilised suwwoundings? How long can we stay? Must we find new lodgings at once?"

"Your father says we may stay here for the rest of the week, thanks to the generosity of the company."

"Oh, hurray!" cried Lexy, and Cecily waltzed up and down the room with her crinoline swirling round her. Then Clem ran in.

"I've had such a breakfast," he shouted, "I'll probably be ill."

"Hush, Clem, calm down," warned his mother. "They don't like noisy little boys in hotels."

Joshua came in, carrying Jamie:

"Mamma, do you realise the greatest blow – the last straw in our losses?" he said heavily, but with a twinkle in his eye. "Baby has lost all his clean napkins, save the two that were in his basket."

"Oh, the poor lamb – " cried Seraphina. "Quickly, Lexy, run out to the haberdashers, will you, and then you and I must start sewing."

And it went on like that all day. At every turn they remembered fresh things that had been lost in the fire and that they simply must have. The morning rehearsal was cancelled so that they could shop, and when they got to the theatre they found that the company had all brought things that they thought might be of use to them. Mrs Tollerton laughingly produced some spare underclothes that she said "Might be cut up to use for Lexy, or indeed for the whole of the family." Lexy sighed, visualising weeks of heavier sewing than ever looming ahead.

"Now, as our friends have all been so thoughtful for us," said Joshua, "I think we should do some good for someone else. Why do we not go to the Institution this afternoon after the rehearsal and visit poor Mrs Bason?"

The family did not show much enthusiasm, but Seraphina said, "Well, perhaps we should, the poor old soul. I'll not take the two little ones, for there is so much infection in those poor-houses."

Clem immediately began to wail, "I want to go to the poor-house, I want to go to the poor-house. Why can't I go if Lexy goes?"

After the rehearsal they left the two little ones in Mrs Tollerton's care and went out to a fruiterer's and bought a basketful of fruit and made their way to the outskirts of the town, where the Institution stood. Lexy felt her heart beating nervously. All her life "the poor-house" had been a dark dread at the back of her mind. Whenever they had been particularly hard up she had heard her mother say, "We shall end up in the poor-house, I know it – I see it."

And occasionally on returning to towns where they had stayed before, they would hear from neighbours who shook their heads sadly that the landlady they were seeking had been "took bad" and had to go into the work-house.

"I don't weally know why we should go to see Mrs Bason," Cecily said, as they approached the dark sinister sprawl of buildings, "for it was in her house that we lost all our belongings. And through her fault – "

"We should go to see her because she is very old and now completely destitute. *We* lost a lot, but we still have our employment safe. Her house was her employment. And that has gone."

"You are right, Joshua," said Seraphina loyally. "But do not you quote Shakespeare to her, now will you? I know you mean it kindly, but it upsets landladies. Especially as she's ill – "

"What a howwid place," cried Cecily, as they reached the iron-spiked gates. "It looks more like a pwison. I'm sure we shall all catch the small-pox." She produced her smelling-salts and sniffed at them ardently. "Lexy, you twy these salts. It will keep away infection."

"No, thank you. They make me choke."

A surly doorkeeper looked at them suspiciously and directed them into a long ward full of small iron beds, in which lay an assortment of very old and very ill women. They tip-toed down the aisle between the beds. There lay Mrs Bason, looking much cleaner and much, much older than she had looked in her own home. Her eyelids flickered recognition at them but she seemed unable to speak. Seraphina bent over her and talked softly to her for a few minutes, and showed her the basket of fruit. The old woman's eyes filled with grateful tears and she just nodded her head. From the other beds eyes were fixed greedily on the basket of fruit. Joshua beckoned one of the attendants, who looked as old and ill as any of the patients.

"Take care that Mrs Bason gets all this fruit herself, if you please."

The attendant also eyed the fruit greedily, and Joshua shrugged his shoulders.

"Come, there is nothing more we can do, and it is unpleasing for the girls," he said to Seraphina.

Lexy bobbed a little curtsey to Mrs Bason, and felt really sorry for her. She wished that they had never joked about her and called her an old witch.

All the eyes above the thin covers watched them as they made their way out. Lexy drew a deep sigh of relief as they came into the open air of the stone courtyard. And then she stopped. For, peeping round every corner were more eyes – young ones this time. Little frail, thinly-clad children were looking round every corner, their eyes enormous in their tiny pinched faces. But every time she looked straight at them, they were gone.

"Oh, Mamma – " breathed Lexy.

"Yes, my dearest, I see them." Seraphina took Lexy's hand and they hurried towards the gate. Cecily was protesting that she felt faint, and that they must stop at an apothecary's for some sal volatile. Outside the gate Lexy hugged her mother's arm.

"Mamma," she said, "Mamma, I'm so glad – so glad that – "

What she wanted to say was that she felt guilty at ever having envied little rich children who lived in proper houses, and had dolls and ponies and fine clothes, and that, having seen the little workhouse children she would never think herself hardly done by again, for she had a mother and father. But this was too complicated to put into words so she finished up with, "I'm so glad about you and Papa."

Joshua was shaking his head and murmuring: "We should not have taken the girls there – " And as they hurried back into the town they were very gay, to try and forget what they had seen. Joshua took them into a coffee shop, to warm them up after the long cold walk, and they drank coffee and ate Bath buns.

The rest of the week passed very pleasantly. Somehow, living at the Red Lion took away the seriousness of their losses in the fire. And it was an excellent week for the theatre. The wealthy people from all over the county supported it, and on the Saturday both houses were full to capacity, with people standing in the gallery. The takings were enough for everyone to have their full salaries, and for Joshua to repay half the sum that the company had given him, although they all tried hard to refuse it.

"There'll be no doubts about the journey this week," said Seraphina gaily. "Why, we could even go first-class if we really wanted to."

"Another fwightful journey," mourned Cecily. "I wish we could stay here for ever."

"You have not seen anything yet, daughter," Joshua told her. "We have been travelling weekly since you joined us. After next week we go on to the fit-up dates. It'll be one-night stands for the next few weeks." Cecily closed her eyes as if in pain.

"But, Papa, you should not have to play the one-night stands – why, you have a weputation – "

"A reputation made in the one-night stands, me girl. I don't despise them. The people in the villages and small

79

towns have as much right to the drama as those in Oldcastle and Marlingford and such. After Huncaster next week, you will see what trouping is really like."

On the journey to Huncaster Lexy discovered that Spring was on the way. From the carriage window she could see the first pale primroses on the railway embankments. Sometimes the train stopped for so long that she felt sure she could get out and pick some and jump in again before it started. But her mother would not hear of it. The coming of Spring meant more than primroses to Lexy. It meant that dressing-rooms and lodgings would not be so chilly, that she would not need to pile her day clothes on top of her counterpane in order to keep warm in bed, and that Jamie would not be so fretful on the long journeys. She waved in a superior manner to some children who were picking primroses by the side of the track, and longingly watching the trains go by.

As usual they had to change at Turnpike Junction. While they were waiting on the platform for the next train, Lexy pulled at her mother's gown.

"Mamma," she said. "There's Wicked Wiling."

Along the platform strolled a tall man with jet black whiskers and flashing black eyes. This was Luke Wiling, an actor-manager with an immense following in the provinces. He toured a repertoire of melodramas, in which he always played the villain, and for this reason had acquired in the profession the nickname of "Wicked". He and Joshua were rivals of long standing, but whereas Joshua had quite a solid reputation as a classical actor, "Wicked Wiling" appealed more to the popular taste. Joshua saw him and grunted: "There is that mountebank – I wonder where they are bound for?" Behind Wiling trailed his company, his skinny wife and four swarthy daughters, and a selection of down-at-heel young men and flashy young women. Courtney Stanton put his nose in the air and remarked to Cecily that because one was in the profession there was no call to think one need not look a gentleman.

"Too twue," agreed Cecily. "It is twoupes such as that which get a bad name for the pwofession."

To their surprise, the Wiling troupe boarded the same train as themselves.

"Well, where can they be playing?" demanded Seraphina. "Beyond Huncaster there are only a few litle villages on this line."

"One-night stands in the villages, doubtless," said Joshua patronisingly. "They never play the big towns. Townsfolk would laugh their nonsense to scorn."

On arriving at Huncaster there was the usual flurry of waking Clem and finding his mittens and muffler, but this was simplified by their lack of luggage. As they stepped on to the platform, who should salute Joshua but Wicked Wiling.

"Ho, there, friend," he cried boisterously. "How do you fare?"

"Well, I thank you," said Joshua politely, raising his hat.

"They must be going on by coach, I suppose," surmised Seraphina, "but where, I cannot think."

"Those hussies!" said Mrs Tollerton, wrapping her ample shawl round herself. "They look worse than ever, I declare."

As they were haggling over cabs and landladies outside the station, Joshua suddenly stopped dead and stared straight in front of him, as he did in Macbeth.

81

"What is it, my precious?" asked Seraphina.

Joshua pointed a dramatic forefinger at a bill pasted on the wall. "Luke Wiling," it read, "and his company of superior players will present each night at the Corn Exchange Hall one of his dramatic pieces, including 'The Haunted Headsman', 'Lady Cathleen's Sacrifice', 'The Pirate Queen' and many others, with music, dances and comedy interludes."

"The Corn Exchange," gasped Joshua, "That was not used as a theatre when last we were here – there was only the Royalty, where we are to play. This is grave news, me dear," he told Seraphina.

"But they will not take away from our business, my precious, for our shows are of a different standard."

"I hope you are correct – " Joshua stroked his chin doubtfully, "but they have their bills out already. Ours are yet to go up. One minute; I must speak to Will."

He was soon deep in consultation with Will, the prompter, while the cab-horse stamped impatiently.

"Come, Joshua, the children are tired," called Seraphina. "Don't fret about that Wiling," she told him when he got into the cab, "he is a ranting fool, not an actor."

"Papa," said Clem, "can I go and see 'The Pirate Queen'?"

"No," said Joshua sharply. "You will not set foot inside the Corn Exchange."

Lexy, too, had secretly been wondering what "The Pirate Queen" was like, but felt rather guilty at such disloyalty.

They were making for the lodgings where they always stayed in Huncaster, at cheerful Widow Chitterworth's with

her large family of boys and girls. The Mannerings always lived in with the family there, and sat down at the immense dining-table that was usually laid for about twenty. Lexy was a bit afraid of the young Chitterworths, who shouted so loudly in their broad northern brogue. They were welcomed by an assortment of them who all exclaimed with delight at Jamie, whom they had not seen before. There was no unpacking to do that evening, as they had so few belongings, so Joshua announced his intention of going out bill-posting, with Will.

"Can I come too, Papa? Can I come too?" pleaded Clem.

"No, Clem. You got paste in your hair the last time," said Seraphina.

"I'll go with him, Mamma, and see that he is good," said Lexy, and so they muffled up and started out. Wherever there was a bill advertising the Wilings' shows, they pasted one of their own bills, next door to it or opposite. Lexy thought that their posters were much more tasteful than their rivals'. They read: "Joshua Mannering presents his London company of actors in a week's season of drama." And underneath were the plays that they performed. By the time they had covered the whole town, Clem and Lexy were dead tired and their hands stiff with the home-made paste that the prompter carried in a little can.

"There – that should cook Mr Wiling's goose," sighed Joshua with satisfaction. "And all quite fair and above-board – side by side, so that all may take their choice."

The little Chitterworths eyed Lexy and Clem enviously when they heard that they had been out bill-posting. There was a large supper of tripe and onions that Cecily voted "disgusting" on first sight, but she eventually put away two platefuls of it.

Next day on the way to the theatre, Joshua pointed out the Corn Exchange.

"Just opposite the Royalty Theatre, you see. It will be a stiff battle for patronage."

"Papa," said Lexy, "did you notice any of our bills on the way?"

"No, my love, but there should be one – let me see, this wall here – " He broke off. On the large expanse of wall at a corner, were two bills of the Wilings, one of them stuck over the Mannerings' bill that had been pasted there the night before.

"The blackguards!" exclaimed Joshua. "So that is their little game, is it? By Jove, we'll beat them at it. As soon as it gets dusk, we'll all go out pasting theirs over. I wonder if it's the same all over the town – "

It was. Not one of the Mannerings' bills had been left. Wiling's bill-posters had done their job well. Fretting and fuming, Joshua led the way to the Royal Theatre. Just as they were about to enter the stage-door, there came the sudden crash of a brass-band striking up.

"Hark, Mamma, a German band!" cried Clem.

Round the corner came a strange procession. Half a dozen musicians in ill-fitting uniforms led it, followed by Wicked Wiling in top-boots, cloak and plumed hat riding on a mangy cart-horse. Next came a gilded chariot drawn by a donkey, and in the chariot, shivering in her draperies in the cold morning air, sat Mrs Wiling dressed as Boadicea. The rest of the company marched behind, some dressed as heralds, some as harlequins and all looking very footsore.

"Barn-stormers!" growled Joshua.

Behind the procession ran a crowd of excited urchins, thrilled at the sight of the play-actors. Seraphina shook her head sadly.

"It's the way to bring in the audience in a town like this," she said.

"I'd love to go in a procession," said Clem. "I'd ride on – on an elephant."

At the theatre the company were full of indignation against the Wilings and some of them had found themselves in the same lodgings as their rivals.

"The sluts," fumed Mrs Tollerton. "They came down to breakfast in wrappers and curl papers."

When Joshua told them what had happened to their posters, there was general indignation.

"We'll all come bill-posting tonight after the show," declared Barney Fidgett. "We'll teach them they can't do that sort of thing."

It was a very thin audience that night, as bad as any Monday night they had had. But outside the theatre were the "House Full" boards, challenging the Corn Exchange to do better.

Before long, "Full House" said the boards outside the Corn Exchange.

"I don't believe it," said Joshua. "They couldn't be full on a Monday. Clem, run across the road and see if you can peep through the doors. If you get caught don't let them know who you are. And don't run straight back to this theatre, saunter around a little."

Before long Clem was back, with shining eyes.

"Papa," he cried, "there was a lady dressed as a pirate and she had a sword and there was a ship, papa, a *real* ship – and what do you think she was doing, Mamma? She was making a gentleman walk the plank!"

"Yes, yes," said Joshua, "but how many were there in the house?"

"It wasn't a house, papa, it was a ship – " Clem's head was still full of the delights he had seen. "Oh, Papa, why can't we do pieces like that?"

"Clem, how many were there in the audience?"

"I counted to fifteen, Papa, and then I went wrong. But there were many more."

"They weren't full, then?"

"Oh, no. And this lady pirate – "

"That is enough, Clem. You have done your work well." And Joshua gave him a halfpenny, which was riches to Clem. He could buy with it enough brandy-balls to make him feel quite pleasantly ill.

All the week there was competition between the two companies. Business appeared to be fairly equally divided between them. The local gentry and the shop-keepers came to see the Mannerings, the factory workers and craftsmen went to the Corn Exchange. But Saturday would decide which company would have had the better week. The Wilings were doing three performances, almost continuously, but the Mannerings were doing only two.

By this time the poster battle had been abandoned. For three nights the Mannerings had gone round pasting their bills back over the ones the Wilings had covered. And each morning the Mannerings' had gone again. Then on the Friday morning they found that their bills had been left alone and felt, at long last, their persistence had borne fruit.

On Saturday, before the first show began, they were all up on the stage peering through chinks in the curtains watching the auditorium fill. It filled steadily, first the gallery, then the pit.

"I believe it will be full," breathed Joshua.

The stream of people continued so that they had to hold the curtain for ten minutes to get everyone safely seated. By the time the curtain went up, the house was packed to capacity.

"I can't understand it," said Joshua, "and with two theatres open – "

The next show was the same. They were packed to capacity.

"Travelling fares, baggage, lodgings, salaries and complete repayment of our debts," breathed Joshua out of the side of his mouth, during the last scene of "A Midsummer-Night's Dream".

"I wonder if the Wilings had as good a day as this," said Joshua as they packed up to go home. "Let us go across and see if we can see any of his company, and we might enquire."

All this good business had put him in such a good humour that he felt no ill-will towards his rival at the moment. They crossed the darkened street and stopped outside the Corn Exchange. It was empty and deserted.

And across each of the boards outside was a slip pasted. On them, in Clem's scrawling hand-writing were the words: "Theatre closed on account of the small-pocks."

"Did I spell it right?" asked Clem innocently.

"Clem," cried Seraphina, horrified, "did *you* do that?"

"Yes," said Clem, "I thought you'd be pleased."

Joshua shook him by the shoulders.

"But what made you think of such a trick?"

"I heard Mr Fidgett and Mr Tollerton talking, and they said that the only thing that would stop people going to see trash of that sort was a small-pox scare."

Cecily trilled with laughter.

"Oh, Papa – you must admit it is funny. They were such a howwid lot of people, too."

"But I want to know what's become of them," said Joshua. "It's quite unnatural for them just to have disappeared like that. Surely they must have discovered the hoax. And if I know Wicked Wiling he'd not be content to leave the score uneven." Joshua stroked his chin thoughtfully. "Now, what can have been the outcome of this?"

The streets were almost deserted but Joshua stopped a woman who was passing by and demanded, "What is this about small-pox? Is there any truth in it?"

She drew away from him nervously.

"Ay, it's in the town, they say. Some play-actors brought it – " She looked speculatively at the Mannerings. "And if I'm not mistaken, you're some of the same ilk."

"But what has become of the troupe who were here at the Corn Exchange?"

"Oh, they're in the jail, to keep them from the rest of the folk who've not got the sickness." And she hurried on.

Cecily burst out laughing again.

"Oh, how dwoll!" she cried. "I'd love to see those flashy cweatures all shut up in the town jail, when they've not got the small-pox at all!"

Joshua was looking worried.

"It's not so much of a joke, me girl," he told her. "I think we'd best go along to the town jail and see that no harm comes to them."

89

Cecily was amazed.

"But, Papa – they are our wivals – our enemies! Is it not a good thing if they are shut up?"

Joshua shook his head.

"It is not fair. I must admit," he smiled a little unwillingly, "it has its comic side, but I cannot see fellow-troupers suffering at the hands of townsfolk for a joke such as this. I will not be cross with Clem – for he thought he was being helpful."

"You are so good, my precious," sighed Seraphina. "You have a noble nature."

They made for the jail, which was in the town hall. Outside, a small crowd was shouting and gesticulating.

"What is the to-do?" demanded Joshua.

"It's the strolling players," growled one man. "They've brought the small-pox to the town. Out with them, say I – drive 'em out of the town. We don't want them in our midst – polluting the air. Out with the vagabonds," he shouted fiercely.

Without a word Joshua mounted the steps of the town hall, with his family trailing behind him. Inside there was commotion. Town officials were hurring hither and thither giving orders and countermanding them again. The beadle of the town, in his cocked hat and breeches, looking very flushed and bothered, came up to Joshua and demanded his business.

"I wish to see the Wilings – the play-actors."

"Can't; they've got the small-pox. They're locked up."

"They have not got the small-pox," said Joshua firmly. "It was all a joke. My little lad here started the

90

rumour. They've no more got the small-pox than you or I. Now, lead me to them."

Joshua's serious countenance and dignified bearing impressed the beadle, and at last he unwillingly led them down some cold stone stairs to the dungeon-like cells in the basement.

There, behind bars in separate cells, were all the members of the Wiling troupe. They were rattling at the locked doors, shouting and cursing and screaming at the jailers. A bewildered little man, holding a black bag, was in deep conversation with a constable.

"I can find no trace of the sickness," he was saying. "They are all in perfectly good health. Not a mark on them."

"Of *course* we're in good health – " cried Wicked Wiling, at the top of his villainous voice. "It's you who're ill – mad – demented. We've not got the small-pox – and never have had – let us out, I say."

Joshua went and spoke softly to the little man, evidently a surgeon, who appeared relieved at the explanation, and told the constable, who sent for the beadle. The beadle appeared, puffing and blowing, and very mistrustful of the whole affair. Everybody tried to explain to him at once, but he could not grasp the situation at all – except that the doctor was saying that there was no infection. At last, with a gesture of giving up completely, he threw open the doors of the cells and allowed the Wilings out.

"But don't let me find any of you in the town tomorrow," were his parting words, "or, by Heaven, I'll put you in the stocks, where all your sort should go."

He included the Mannerings in this announcement. Rather sheepishly they all filed out of a back door to avoid the angry crowd and stood awkwardly in the lane looking at each other.

"I'd give a fortune to find the villain who pasted those notices outside the Exchange," said Wiling with an oath.

"I think, Papa," said Clem, "it's my bed-time."

CHAPTER 6

Lexy Goes to School

With the coming of the Spring, the Mannerings resumed a more vagabond existence. They were playing the 'fit-up' dates now; one night only in each town or village. They moved so quickly from place to place that most of the time Lexy could not have told you where they were. Sometimes they played in village halls, occasionally in large rooms or in public houses and once even in a barn. This disgusted Cecily considerably.

"When the girls at the Misses Dingwaters' used to tease me by calling me 'barn-stormer', I was vewy angwy but now I see that they were wight."

She sniffed and gave such a bad performance as Juliet that the rabble in the back rows threw orange peel at her.

Sometimes their lodgings were bad, sometimes they were good. There was the kind landlady in a Cumberland village who had cut down one of her own dresses to fit Lexy – a lovely blue velveteen. So now her tartan dress could descend from the position of "Sunday best" to "every day". But the innkeeper at the next village stole the box in which Joshua had put the night's takings and that made a bad week for everybody.

"Take heart," said Joshua, when his company began to flag, "perhaps, who knows, in one of these villages we may kindle a spark in the breast of some future Milton, a Garrick or a Sheridan – "

"If we could kindle a spark in the grate of our lodgings, it would be a blessing," said Seraphina on one occasion. "The baby's starved with cold."

In one small town where they played, Lexy was stopped by the well-meaning lady of the manor, who asked her all about the life of a play-actor's child.

"What a lucky little girl," she exclaimed. "Nothing to do all day, no lessons, and then playing at night."

Lexy opened her mouth to say: "Nothing to do? Why I'm first to rise in the morning – I look after baby, get the breakfast ready if it's to be done, get the family to rehearsal in time, hold the book to hear people's lines, iron the costumes, pack the skips, lace the actresses' dresses, run out to fetch pies and porter for the actors – " But suddenly as she began to speak she realised that this benevolent lady would never understand; that they might live centuries and centuries apart, for all the understanding that they could have of each other, so instead she just smiled and said meekly, "Yes, Ma'am," and the lady gave her a tract about a mission to the Africans.

Cecily, too, was beginning to worry about her little sister's lack of schooling, and one day when she discovered that Lexy did not know what was the capital of Russia, she spoke strongly on the subject to her parents.

"It's a disgwace," she said, "to have the child twamping about the countwyside like a gipsy – You gave *me* a good education, Papa, so why not Lexy? I declare it makes me ashamed to have a sister with the education of a pauper.''

Joshua shook his head sadly. "I am well aware of my shortcomings over my little Lexy," he said. "I hoped to be able to do as well for all my children as I did for my first-born, but Fate decrees otherwise. To me, however, Lexy seems to be well advanced for her age – ''

He looked thoughtfully at Lexy who was sitting quietly in a corner of the dressing-room, hemming a new overall for Clem.

"She reads and writes well – ''

"I don't want to go to school, Papa," Lexy assured him, "truly I don't – ''

"*I* never cared much for school," put in Seraphina, who sat at the mirror smoothing on her powder with a hare's foot. "I didn't mind the other girls, but the school-marms – oh, they were such crabs – I decided to leave when I was nine."

"Lexy, what did you say was the capital of Wussia?" demanded Cecily, to prove her point.

"Strasbourg – '' said Lexy, shamefacedly.

Joshua exclaimed with horror.

"My child – I did not realise to what extent I had neglected your education. What are seven times nine?"

Completely taken aback, Lexy's mind went blank and she just sat there blushing.

"Why it's fifty-three, isn't it?" said Seraphina, help-fully, "or is it fifty-four? – I can never remember – ''

"You see, Papa?" said Cecily triumphantly. "Lexy is as ignowant as a monkey. She *must* go to school."

"Indeed I fear she must," said Joshua, "but where – and when?"

"Why can't *I* go to school?" chimed in Clem. "Why can't *I* go to school?"

"Hush, Clem, you're only a baby," Seraphina quietened him, anxious not to lose him as well as Lexy to the "school-marms".

"Why, when we finish these howwible one-night stands," said Cecily, "Lexy can go to a diffewent school evewy week, or half-week – She should get an exceedingly vawied education in that way."

Lexy gazed imploringly at her father, hoping that he would have pity on her, but no –

"Yes," he agreed, "Cecily is right. The next time we stay in a town for more than a few days Lexy shall go to school."

For the next few weeks Lexy lived in fear and trembling, expecting to be dispatched to some strange school at any moment, but they were moving so constantly from place to place, and presenting such varied bills that her parents had no chance to think any more about the matter. But then came the day when they arrived in a town to play for a whole week – the first time for months. As they made their way to the lodgings where the Mannerings always stayed in the town of Nessingham, they passed a neat red brick villa which bore a brass plate saying "Mrs Honeywell's School for Young Gentlefolk". Cecily stopped dead in her tracks.

"Mamma! Papa!" she cried. "See – the vewy thing for Lexy. She can go there for a whole week."

"No, no!" said Lexy urgently, taking Cecily's arm, and trying to drag her on. "It would be too expensive. And besides it says 'gentlefolk' and we are play-actors."

"Fiddlededee!" said Cecily, tossing her head. "I am

sure I'm as much a lady as Mrs Honeywell. It's not a patch on the Misses Dingwaters' Academy. I'll take you wound there this evening as soon as you've washed the smuts from your face."

"But can we afford it, my precious?" asked Seraphina anxiously.

"Of course, Mamma. It won't cost much just for the week."

"But I don't want to go to school – " Lexy was nearly in tears. "I've got nothing to wear and I'm frightened of a lot of schoolgirls – and I don't know anything except plays and such."

"Sufficient reason for you to start attending school, me girl," said Joshua.

After they had had a meal at the lodgings and Lexy had put Jamie to bed, Cecily took hold of her firmly and insisted on washing her neck and face and ears with soap and sponge, and very cold water from the china jug on the wash-stand. Then she combed her hair, making tears of pain come into Lexy's eyes when the tangles were tugged. One side of her fringe was rebellious, and would stick up instead of lying flat on her forehead, so Cecily smoothed it down with some damp soap. Lexy was already wearing her new blue velveteen "Sunday best", so there was nothing for her to change into, but Cecily put on her very best gown, the mauve silk, that was now getting a little the worse for wear after so many packings and unpackings.

"Your wrap is shabby, Lexy," Cecily criticised, "you weally must coax Papa into buying you a new one."

"I don't care to, when business is so bad," said Lexy.

Cecily laughed lightly.

"Business is always bad according to Papa – or any

other gentleman, come to that. Gentlemen must be coaxed if we women are ever to have a new bonnet or gown. Leave it to me – I'll tell him you *must* have a new wrap for going to school. Now, are you weady?"

They went swiftly along the street in the dusk, with Cecily holding Lexy's hand very tightly, and rather high up so that her arm began to ache.

"Now Lexy, you must be seen and not heard. I shall talk to Mrs Honeywell. You must just curtsey as we go in and when we come out – for the west, just keep your head up but your eyes down. And don't fidget. And Lexy – turn out your toes – you are walking like a pigeon."

"But I feel like a duck when I turn them out," Lexy objected.

"Hush, we're here now." Cecily gave several nervous coughs as they opened the gate of Mrs Honeywell's house, and Lexy saw that she was pursing her lips into the "Prunes and prisms" shape that the Misses Dingwater had prescribed.

Mrs Honeywell's house was a new red brick villa with neat curtains and a neat front garden where the flowers seemed to blossom in neat regimental formation. There was a long bell-pull on the front door which Cecily pulled timidly at first, then, as nothing happened, a little bit harder, and this time it clanged so loudly and impertinently through the house that Lexy almost turned and ran away.

"Cover your teeth up, Lexy," said Cecily, in the pause that followed. And then the door was opened by a tiny servant girl about Lexy's height.

"Oh, might we have the pleasure of waiting on Mrs Honeywell?" began Cecily in her most refined accents.

But the girl shook her head dolefully: "No, ma'am, that you can't. She's been dead this ten year."

Lexy giggled a little hysterically, and a figure loomed up behind the servant girl.

"You may laugh, child – but she was my mother – " it said. Lexy wished she could have sunk through the floor.

"I'm sorry, ma'am – I didn't know – I mean it sounded funny," Lexy tried to explain, but it only seemed to make it worse. Cecily kicked her sharply on the ankle, and she faded weakly into silence.

"Hepzibah, light the lamp," came the other voice again.

While the maid was struggling with lucifers and an oil lamp, Lexy tried to make out who was speaking. All that she could see was a vast figure looming in the doorway. Then the lamp began to glow, and the girl held it near the door so that it shone on to Cecily and Lexy. Cecily immediately smiled sweetly and said, "Please forgive my little sister – she is so naïve – youth, you know – she meant no offence – "

"An idle tongue – " was the comment.

Now a beam of light fell on to the speaker. She was an enormous woman with a tiny head, wearing a voluminous skirt, so that the final effect was almost triangular. Perched on the apex of the triangle was a tiny lace cap over a hard face with shrewd, enquiring eyes that were weighing up Lexy and Cecily. She seemed to find something strange about them.

"Your sister, you said?"

"Yes, ma'am. I've bwought her to ask if she may come to your school – that is, if there be a school here now – ?"

"By all means there is. My mother, the late Mrs Honeywell, God rest her soul, began it twenty years ago. Now that she has passed over I try to carry on the good work. Needle-work, languages and painting in water-colours extra, of course."

"Of course!" Cecily echoed her eagerly.

"Well, you'd best step inside. Hepzibah, light the lamp in the parlour."

The parlour was the cleanest room Lexy had ever seen – very different from the shoddy lodgings and the rickety splendour of the theatres which had been her only surroundings up till now. The antimacassars were placed with geometrical precision on the backs of the horse-hair armchairs and the sofa, and there was a strong smell of linseed polish. On the mantelpiece stood a large vase of wax flowers in a glass case that Lexy thought very splendid. The only indication that it was a school was the globe of the world that stood in a corner. Globes had always fascinated Lexy, and she could not help putting out a finger and touching it so that it revolved silently.

"Fingers off, miss!" snapped Miss Honeywell, adding with satisfaction, "That globe has just been polished. Sit down, won't you?"

Cecily sat on a lower chair arranging her skirts in a ladylike fashion to cover her feet and ankles. Lexy stood close to her and tried not to fidget.

"I have come to ask you, Mrs – er – Miss Honeywell, if my sister may join your school. It is – er – just for the week, you know."

"The week!" exclaimed Miss Honeywell, her eyebrows shooting up under her cap.

Lexy stared hard at the Indian carpet.

100

"Yes, ma'am. We are on a visit to – " Suddenly Cecily forgot what town they were in.

"Nessingham – " Lexy prompted her in a stage whisper, through sheer force of habit.

"To Nessingham, that's wight – Oh, mercy, I shall forget my own name next – " She laughed gaily, but Miss Honeywell did not stir a muscle.

"We are on a visit with Mamma and Papa, and they do not wish Alexandwa to miss any schooling."

"What schooling has she had, may I ask?" asked Miss Honeywell, looking hard at Lexy, who immediately wanted to curl up like a caterpillar.

"Mostly pwivate tuition," said Cecily airily, and Lexy blushed to her ears to hear her sister telling such stories. "She's a little backward in some subjects, I fear, but in others you'll find her satisfactowy."

"And what extras would you wish her to take?"

"Oh – needlework, perhaps, and – Fwench – I myself was at the Misses Dingwaters' at Tonbwidge. You've heard of the establishment, perhaps?"

Miss Honeywell evidently had, for her manner began to thaw towards Cecily, but she still eyed Lexy with mistrust.

"Very well!" she said eventually. "On Monday, then, at eight o'clock."

"What a terrible time to go to school!" thought Lexy.

"And she will bring her own overall and luncheon basket."

"Thank you, Miss Honeywell. And – er – the financial settlement?"

Miss Honeywell dismissed this abruptly. "A bill will be sent – a proportion of our usual fees, adjusted suitably for such a short period. Hepzibah, show the ladies out."

When they were outside Lexy took hold of Cecily's arm. "Cecily – dear Cecily – " she pleaded, "please don't make me go there. She's *such* a dragon. I know I'll not be happy there."

"Nonsense!" cried Cecily cheerfully. "She's a lady born and bwed. One can see that. She'll soon have you in shape. No more of your behaving like a gipsy child."

Lexy played a game to herself on the walk home that she really *was* a gipsy's child, and would be rolling off next day in a beautiful painted van, away from the horrors of Mrs Honeywell's School for Young Gentlefolk.

Next morning she had to be up at six to get everything done in time. The family were catering for themselves this week, and there was breakfast to be cooked on the range belonging to the friendly landlady, who would keep delaying Lexy by telling long childhood reminiscences of when she was Lexy's age, all in so thick a brogue that Lexy could hardly understand a word. She had just about reached her confirmation when Lexy was ready to carry the breakfast up to her parents' room, so she left the good lady to her tale and when she returned to fetch the warm milk for Jamie, the story was still not finished.

The only person who showed any sympathy for Lexy was her mother. "Don't fret about the school-marms," she whispered in her ear as she kissed her goodbye. "They're a lot of sour old maids, every one. And they can't hurt you."

Seraphina had actually gone to the trouble of packing up a sandwich luncheon for Lexy in an old make-up cabinet of her own, and with this tucked under her arm, Lexy set off by herself for her first day at school.

As she drew near the gate her steps became slower and slower. There was a stream of girls and boys approaching the red brick villa, but each of them was attended by a parent or a maid or a nurse. She was the only one to arrive alone. At the gate she stopped dead and would have turned tail altogether, had not a flurry of school-children and nurses swept her in along with them. All the children stared at her curiously and Lexy wondered if her bonnet seemed too shabby beside theirs. On the doorstep stood Miss Honeywell, looking even larger than she had done in the dark. She was greeting each child with a word of criticism.

"Charles, do not shuffle your feet! Virginia, your bonnet strings are untied!"

Each of the children curtsied or bowed as they sidled past her.

"Oho – " she said loudly, on seeing Lexy, "our new pupil – " Lexy made a rather clumsy bob that would have disgraced her in her father's eyes, had she done it on the stage. "I do not remember your name. What did your sister tell me it was?"

"Alexandra Mannering," she murmured.

"Speak up – speak up!"

Countless pairs of eyes were fastened interestedly on Lexy and she heard one half-suppressed giggle.

"I said, Alexandra Mannering," she repeated, louder this time.

Miss Honeywell clucked her large teeth disapprovingly. "Tut! tut! That will never do. You should not say 'I said Alexandra Mannering' in that pert tone. It should be, 'Alexandra Mannering, if you please, ma'am.' Now child, what is your name?"

"You've just said it," Lexy told her wonderingly. Immediately all the children clustering around broke into

103

shrill peals of piercing laughter. Miss Honeywell turned on them angrily.

"Silence!" she thundered. "You will all write out 'Children should be seen and not heard' thirty times after school."

The children's faces fell, and they turned and shambled off.

"You would do well not to gape, miss," she told Lexy. Lexy obediently covered up her teeth. Then Miss Honeywell barked, "Follow me," and turned into the room in which they had been interviewed the previous night. There were now rows of school desks in the room, and the children were ranged in these according to size, with the smallest in front, facing the globe which stood beside a table at which Miss Honeywell sat. The children were of all ages and shapes and sizes, but there seemed to be a large number of girls of about Lexy's age. They all stared hard at her, and she was miserably conscious of her straight shoulder-length hair with a fringe, and their beautiful ringlets of gold or brown.

Miss Honeywell produced a large book and started to call out the names of the class.

"Present, please, ma'am," they each replied. Lexy kept rehearsing this over to herself, but couldn't quite understand what it meant. Surely they were not asking the stern Miss Honeywell to give them presents? For some reason she expected her name to come at the end, and was surprised when it was included under the Ms. At first she could only nod feebly, but then managed to croak, "Present, please, ma'am."

When the list was finished, Miss Honeywell went to a corner cupboard and produced some books.

"Oh," thought Lexy, "these must be the presents they were talking about."

But they turned out merely to be lesson books. And then she realised her stupid mistake. Of course the class had not been asking Miss Honeywell for gifts – that had been what was called "taking the register". She had heard about it from Cecily. She blushed for shame at her ignorance.

The first lesson was reading, and they each read a paragraph in turn. Lexy was appalled. They droned away, stumbling and stopping and spelling out the words, even great girls of eleven and twelve. If her father had been there, Lexy dared not imagine what he would have said. The book they were reading was dull enough, but at least they might make it sound like sense. When it came to her turn she stood up and started off quite confidently. Ever since she was about four she had had to pore over books, learning lines, hearing other people's parts, and prompting, and it was all an easy matter for her. But no sooner had she begun than Miss Honeywell put her hands over her ears as if in pain and said, "Not so loudly, Alexandra! A more lady-like tone, if you please."

So Lexy sank her voice to the level of the mumblings of the other children, and somehow this made the passage she was reading sound extremely dramatic and rather interesting.

"The main products of this part of India," she read with an air of mystery, "are hemp, tea, rice, *and* – " She paused for effect, "all manner of spices."

The class burst out laughing again.

"Sit down, Alexandra," said Miss Honeywell. "I do not like to think that you meant to be impertinent."

Lexy sat down abashed. How could Miss Honeywell think she meant to be impertinent, when she was trying to read her very best and also to make the subject a little more interesting?

The next lesson was needlework, and each little girl brought out a sampler on which she was embroidering the most complicated patterns and pictures in cross-stitch. Lexy had never sewn a sampler in her life. She had always been far too busy hemming and seaming stage costumes and clothes for herself and her small brothers. And so it was rather clumsily that she began to write her name in cross-stitch on the square of crash she was given. The little boys were making kettle-holders of thick felt with brightly-coloured wools, and Lexy thought that this looked much more fun, and certainly it was more useful. The sewing lesson seemed to go on for ever. Miss Honeywell read aloud to them from Gibbon's "Decline and Fall of the Roman Empire", breaking off every few minutes with, "Willie, do not put your thread in your mouth – " "No whispering on the back bench please – "

And then the big clock on the mantelpiece struck eleven and Miss Honeywell told them to fetch their wraps and they might walk in the garden for five minutes. The garden was not very big. It had a small lawn in the middle with paths surrounding it, and along the paths they had to promenade, two-by-two in a crocodile.

Lexy found herself walking with a plump, flaxen-haired girl dressed in a shiny satin dress, who looked just like a wax doll.

"Why is your hair so strange?" she asked Lexy. "Why do you not have it in curls?"

"I do – on Sundays," said Lexy.

"You don't come from these parts, do you?"

"Well – no – "

"And where you come from do all the girls wear their hair so?"

"A few – Yes, some do – "

Lexy was totally unable to explain why she wore her hair in this page-boy's fashion, as she did not wish to own to being a play-actor's child, for Cecily had warned her that she must not do so or her life would be unbearable at school.

"It took me thwee terms to live it down at the Misses Dingwaters'," Cecily had told her.

Lexy found it very dull marching round and round and kept thinking of all the things she ought to be doing at the theatre. She was sure that Cecily would not bother to iron her gown for the evening's performance. And little Jamie would be neglected and there would be no one to look after the prompting in the rehearsal – She sighed deeply.

"Have you got the colic?" demanded the doll-like girl beside her.

"No," said Lexy, "I was only thinking – "

"What does your Papa do?" the girl continued. Lexy thought quickly.

"He is – a speaker," she said at last.

"With a magic lantern, I suppose?" Lexy made no reply and the girl went on regardlessly, "Isn't Miss Honeywell an old dragon? I declare she gets worse every day. I am to leave school next year and go to Switzerland to be finished," she added proudly. "The other girls say that you have never been to school before. Is that truly so?"

"Yes," said Lexy shamefacedly.

"You had a governess then? Your Papa must be very

rich, I suppose. But why does he not buy you proper clothes for school?"

Lexy was saved the embarrassment of answering by the appearance of Miss Honeywell at the door of the house ringing a tiny bell in one enormous hand.

For the rest of the morning they did Arithmetic. Miss Honeywell chalked up problems on the blackboard and they had to write down the answers on their slates. Lexy was quite good at figures in a practical way. It was always she who counted the change in shops, and discovered if the shop-keepers were trying to cheat them. But these obscure questions about boys dividing apples into eighths and six-teenths and giving them away did not seem at all possible. From her experience of her own brother, boys were more likely to eat the whole apple themselves and then ask for bites from their sisters'. She tried drawing large, round apples and dividing them up in order to calculate the answer, and while she was doing this a heavy hand descended upon her shoulder.

"Alexandra Mannering!" came Miss Honeywell's bass voice. "So you have time for drawing pictures – I presume you have found the answers to the problems?"

"Why, no, I was just – "

"Silence. Give me your slate."

Miss Honeywell took the slate and surveyed it icily.

"Not one answer – Nothing but idle drawings. Alex-andra Mannering – you are to stand on the dunce's stool."

A gasp of horror went round the class-room. Lexy thought that the dunce's stool must be some horrible torture. She was surprised to find that it was only an ordi-nary three-legged wooden stool that Miss Honeywell drew into the centre of the room.

"Come here, Miss Mannering, if you please."

Lexy went and climbed on to the stool and Miss Honeywell placed on her head a tall cone-shaped hat with a large D on it. All the other girls were watching with fascinated eyes. But Lexy was so bewildered by all that had happened since the morning that she could no longer even feel confused. After all, she had stood for so many hours on so many stages perfectly still, holding things, with strange hats on, and certainly with a few more people than this staring at her – So she fixed her gaze on the leaves of the apple-tree outside the window, that was just going to blossom, and started to go through her lines for a new comedy that they were putting into the bill as an after-piece. Her composure seemed to annoy Miss Honeywell.

"A sense of shame is befitting to a Christian child," she suddenly announced. Lexy jumped at the suddenness of this, and felt that some remark was called for.

"Just as you say, ma'am," she said, and the class rocked with silent laughter. Miss Honeywell's face flamed.

"You will remain behind after school is over this afternoon, and write out what I have just said fifty times. Now you may leave the dunce's stool. It is time for luncheon."

Their lunch was eaten in the tiny garden, sitting on benches, and consuming the contents of their own baskets. Lexy's was greatly admired, for, being an old theatrical make-up box it consisted of three tiers that could be pulled up and back on a sort of trellis, so that each tray displayed its contents in steps. The girls began to look at her with a little more respect.

"I did laugh when you stood up to the old dragon

like that," said the plump girl she had walked with mid-morning.

"Stood up to her?" Lexy could not understand how her behaviour had been at all remarkable.

It was very pleasant sitting out in the garden after the stuffy class-room, and Lexy began to think if it were always like this, with the girls beginning to be a little friendly, perhaps school would not be too bad.

But then Miss Honeywell and the horrid little bell appeared again, and her heart sank.

"Girls only – Girls only – " she was calling, and the girls filed in all looking very miserable.

"Back-boards!" one of them whispered to Lexy. Lexy had heard about back-boards from Cecily, for they had been a very important part of the curriculum at the Misses Dingwaters'. The boards were strapped across the girls' backs to make them sit up straight and to give them good poise and carriage. Lexy found it most uncomfortable and the straps cut into her painfully. After they had sat in perfect silence for some time, Miss Honeywell said, "And now we will do book-balancing."

Lexy thought that this was more Arithmetic, but no.

"This," Miss Honeywell explained, producing some heavy volumes, "will teach you to be graceful, like the Eastern women who carry jars on their heads."

Round and round the room they sailed, balancing the heavy books. Lexy found it easy, for the top of her head was fairly flat, but the other girls stumbled and dropped their books, and Miss Honeywell scolded. Lexy got tired of ordinary walking so she did a few little dancing steps. Miss Honeywell turned on her sharply.

"Alexandra Mannering! You are being frivolous. Kindly walk in step – "

Lexy wisely made no reply to this. She was learning that at school, silence was the safest refuge.

Then the little boys were brought in. Lexy thought

111

it very unfair that they should be allowed the extra play-time just because girls were expected to learn deportment.

The afternoon was spent on a drawing and painting lesson. Miss Honeywell placed on her desk a vase of spring flowers, and each child was given a box of colours and a brush and told to copy them. Lexy had never tried to paint on such a small scale before. She had very often lent a hand with the scenery, and enjoyed slapping on the paint with giant brushes, but this little flower study was fidgeting work. However, she tried very hard, and was really getting interested in it when suddenly her hair received a sharp tug from behind. She swung round to see who had pulled it, and in doing so she knocked the little round jar of painting water on her desk. It ran all over the picture and dripped down to the Indian carpet. There was a gasp of horror from her neighbours that brought Miss Honeywell to the spot in a hurry. She opened her mouth and Lexy saw the words, "Alexandra Mannering – " forming, so she hastily put in, "I beg your pardon, ma'am, but somebody behind me – "

"Silence!" thundered Miss Honeywell. "Carelessness and slovenliness are bad enough by themselves – but tale-telling I will not have in my school."

"But I was not telling tales – I was telling the truth – "

"Do not argue – Do you not know that young people should be seen and not heard? You will mop up the painting water from the carpet, and you will stay in when the other children have gone and write out the maxim I have just mentioned."

"Will that be *after* all the others have written it out thirty times, and I have written out the other one fifty times?" Lexy enquired, remembering the threats of the morning. The other children hissed audibly at this remark, and Lexy realised that she would be exceedingly unpopular for reminding the teacher. But she only wanted to get things straight.

"I have decided that the other students may forgo their punishments," said Miss Honeywell icily. "They have worked hard all day. But from you, Miss, we have had nothing but idleness and impertinence."

Lexy eyes filled with tears. She had tried so hard all day, and it had turned out so badly.

When the end of lessons arrived and the other children were putting on their bonnets and wraps, Miss Honeywell brought her a slate and slate pencil and told her to begin. Just as the last of the children was about to depart, the pretty fair-haired girl that Lexy had fancied might become her friend, approached her and whispered coldly. "You're a tittle-tattle! We don't want your sort here!"

Lexy sat stunned as though she had been hit.

"Come along, Miss. You'll never finish your task at this rate," snapped Miss Honeywell.

Alone in the empty class-room, Lexy wrote out her lines and every time she had filled her slate, Miss Honeywell appeared and rubbed it all out, so that she had to start again. It grew later and later and she began to worry about whether she would be in time for the show. From the basement below came a rattle of crockery as though Miss Honeywell's meal was being prepared. The sun had stopped shining in at the window.

When Miss Honeywell had not visited her for some length of time, Lexy cautiously tip-toed to the door. The hall was quite empty. She found her wrap and her bonnet and luncheon box, and walked noiselessly to the front door.

The latch was very heavy, and she had difficulty in opening it, and as she ran out and down the steps, the door banged loudly behind her.

Lexy ran like the wind. It was so wonderful to be free at last that the relief made her cry, and she ran sobbing with tears streaming down her face, through the main streets of Nessingham. It was a long time since they had played in this town, but with the instinct of a homing pigeon she made for the theatre. Down through the market place, into the main square – There it was, standing like a fortress – a shabby stucco fortress – with the Mannerings' bills flapping outside. Down the narrow alley she ran – A gas lamp flared over the dark little doorway. She ran in, nodding to the stage-door keeper, and made her way down under the stage to the small dank dressing-rooms. She flung open the door of the first one she came to, and there they were, miraculously the same and incredibly dear to her at this moment.

Seraphina was putting her make-up on, with Jamie lying crying across her knees. Cecily was leaning over her mother's shoulders and getting in her way to try and get the best reflection in the mirror. Joshua, with Clem on his shoulder, was striding up and down the room repeating his lines. Lexy stood gasping and choking in the doorway.

"Papa!" she cried. "I'm sorry to be so late – Mamma – Mamma – "

She ran and buried her face in her mother's shoulder, catching the familiar odour of lavender water and grease-paint. "They kept me in – They said I was a tittle-tattle – Oh, Mamma – I needn't go back, need I?"

Instantly Jamie was replaced in his basket, and Seraphina's smooth arms were round her.

"Of course you needn't, mother's lamb – Why, we've been in such a state without you."

"Mercy, yes," agreed Cecily. "My costume is a disgwace – all cweased and cwumpled. And Jamie's been sick all day, and Clem has been wicked past all belief – "

Lexy lifted a tear-stained face to her father. "Then Papa – Need I go back tomorrow? Need I?"

Joshua looked at her with a twinkle in his eyes under the dark brows.

"If the troupe cannot do without you, daughter, I do not think you should. Now – put on your make-up with all good speed."

"And then, *please* dear Lexy, iron my dwess. I'm sowwy you've had such a wetched day – "

"And darling child, just change Jamie, will you? He's fretting so – "

"And you'll be on the book for the first act, will you not?"

"Oh, yes, Papa – Very well, Cecily – Come, Clem, stop plaguing Papa – "

And Lexy knew that she was back in her element – back where she belonged – in a theatre – so long as they were all there together.

CHAPTER 7

Fever Town

It was very hot in the train. The windows would not open, and the six Mannerings and Mr and Mrs Tollerton were crammed into one carriage. Lexy, sitting next to Gertrude Tollerton, with Jamie on her knee, was being squashed unbearably between the bulk of the character woman and the hard wooden corner of the compartment. The sun beat unmercifully through the window, and Clem kept threatening to be sick.

"And we're going to Scanchester – " thought Lexy despairingly.

Scanchester was one of the largest of the northern industrial towns, and was certainly the dirtiest. They had never found good lodgings at Scanchester and audiences were usually poor. Lexy hated the blackness of the city and the overpowering scurry of the streets, which were usually shrouded in a yellow fog whenever she had been there. But this time it was very different weather. There was a serious drought hanging over the north. It had not rained for two months, and water was scarce, and nearly non-existent in some of the towns and villages they had been visiting. Their business had suffered, for people were not anxious to come indoors on evenings like this. They preferred to stay in the open air, longing for a cool evening breeze. The Mannerings, in their heavy Shakespearean costumes and theatrical make-up, had suffered agonies of suffocation every night. Clem had horrified one provincial audience by coming on to the stage as Puck clad only in his drawers.

"Mercy on us!" sighed Seraphina, dabbing eau-de-cologne on her temples. "We shall melt before we get to Scanchester."

"Scanchester!" groaned Matthew Tollerton. "I detest the very name of the town. It was at Scanchester I was booed when I played my first leading part. It was at Scanchester that I lost my dear old father. It was at Scanchester my own troupe was finally disbanded."

"But, my love," Gertrude reminded him, "have you forgotten? We were married at Scanchester!"

"Yes," said Matthew Tollerton.

At this moment the train drew up at a tiny wayside halt, and a very old and very dirty Irishwoman in a red flannel petticoat carrying a large basket, crammed herself into the compartment. She had to stand swaying amongst their knees as the train started again. Joshua rose and offered his seat with a gentlemanly bow. Lexy thought with a glow of pride how perfect her father's manners were, for not by the flicker of an eyelid had he shown any annoyance at having to give up his seat.

"Blessings, yer honour," cried the old woman, and sank heavily into the seat on to the edge of Cecily's skirt. Cecily drew it away hastily and immediately brought out her smelling-salts. It was on occasions like these that Lexy felt she would have liked to slap her sister.

117

As soon as she was seated, the Irishwoman started to talk.

"Sure an' these are terrible times we do be livin' in. What with the heat and the drought and the fever a woman don't know if she'll be seein' another morning's loight."

Everyone murmured rather embarrassed agreement. Then Mr Tollerton suddenly sat up with a serious face and leant across to the woman.

"The fever, did you say?"

The woman lifted her brown gnarled hands in horror. "Sure, by the saints, and it's the truth I'm tellin'. In the city it do be ragin'. Two thousand poor bodies laid in the graveyard these past weeks gone."

"In Scanchester?"

"It's the truth, my lady, as God lives, and I trust you'll not be goin' there with these little ones?"

Seraphina's face had paled. There was a silence and then she said weakly, "Yes, that's where we're bound, I fear."

"The saints have mercy on you this night," cried the Irishwoman, lifting her eyes to heaven. "Let you turn back, my sirs and ladies, and not go near the wicked city that's paying for its sinful ways by this plague."

"Good lady," said Joshua politely, although his face was tense, "we perforce must continue our journey, for our work lies at Scanchester. We are a troupe of players and are booked to perform at the theatre."

"Play-actors, is it?" she cried, her eyes widening further. "And ye look like God-fearin' critters."

"And so we are, madam," said Joshua, containing his feelings, "and grateful for your warning. But I'm afraid there is no turning back for us."

"Why does that lady talk so funnily?" Clem now demanded, and had to be kept quiet with biscuits. At the next village halt, the Irishwoman, who had been eyeing them with intense suspicion, rose and got out of the compartment.

"Do you turn back," were her last words, "lest the wrath of God descend on you, and you livin' in evil ways the while." And she was gone.

Lexy shivered suddenly. Cecily spread out her skirts and said petulantly, "What a fwightful old woman. Twying to scare us with her old wives' tales. Fever, indeed! Evil ways! The impertinence!"

But Joshua and Seraphina were exchanging worried looks.

"It does not come as a surprise to hear that there is fever in Scanchester," said Joshua gravely, "they are usually afflicted every summer, and this summer – with the drought – " He left the sentence unfinished.

"Will I catch the fever?" demanded Clem, "and die young and go to heaven like in 'Little Sir Randolph'?"

"You won't die young!" Gertrude Tollerton told him. "You're too much of a young limb."

"Hush, Clem, that is idle talk," said Joshua.

Lexy hugged Jamie, to stop herself thinking grim thoughts, and he cried because it made him too warm.

"Mamma, is there no milk left, or water even, for Jamie to have a sip?" she asked.

"No, my love. The flask is empty. I could only get a drop, you know. I don't know what's to become of the poor lamb."

Soon they began to pass through the grim outskirts of Scanchester. The crowded, tumbledown houses seemed to become blacker as they approached the centre of the city. In the sky there was a fiery glow from the furnaces and the tall chimneys towered threateningly above the railway station as they thankfully got out of the train. There was not a breath of air. The platform seemed rather deserted, and the passengers descending from the train looked about them in a bewildered manner. There was not a porter to be seen, and no-one even bothered to collect their tickets. There was not a cab to be found, and there were no landladies waiting for possible lodgers. The Tollertons and the Mannerings parted company, as the Tollertons had lodgings at which they always stayed when at Scanchester.

When they were alone, Joshua turned to the rest of his family and said sadly, "I fear that we must find lodgings in the meanest quarter of the town."

"That is no novelty for us," said Seraphina, but without bitterness.

Leaving some of their baggage in the station cloakroom they trudged off, carrying their hand luggage. All the streets were deserted, and there seemed to be not a breath of air in them. It was like walking in a vacuum. The drains and gutters were full of refuse, as there had been no rain to sluice them clean, and the whole town smelt unhealthily.

"What a stink!" observed Clem.

"Clem!" his mother rebuked him. "You should say: 'it is somewhat close, is it not?' "

"It isn't close. It stinks."

"I am inclined to agree with Clem," Joshua said wryly.

"Papa, must we really stay here if there is fever about?" whined Cecily. Joshua did not bother to answer.

When they were at last in a narrow street lined with

tumbledown houses, Joshua said, "I fear that this must suffice for the present. I will see which houses have accommodation."

The first door at which he knocked was not opened. Instead two wide frightened eyes appeared at a square flap cut in the wood, and a dread whisper came, in answer to his question, "Nay. You'd best go away, sir. There's the fever here."

Joshua backed away and lifted his hat.

"God be with you," he said, and the melancholy eyes filled with tears.

This terrified Lexy, and she clung to her mother's arm.

"Mamma, Mamma – Is it all right for us here?"

"Why, yes, my precious. We're all strong and healthy, not sickly gutter urchins, like these people. The fever always hits the poorest classes, you know."

"Then why must we stay in a poor street?"

"You know why, my lamb."

At last they found a house that would take them in for a very few shillings a week if they provided their own food. The woman seemed very absent-minded, and merely said, "It's oopstairs. Two rooms. Four beds – " and then disappeared into the bad-smelling rear regions of the house.

The rooms were quite the worst they had stayed in for some time, with low ceilings and broken windows stopped up with dirty rags. Seraphina sang old burlesque numbers to cheer herself up as she unpacked. Joshua hardly seemed to notice the state of the rooms.

"I must go to the theatre immediately," he said, and disappeared.

The bed-linen was so dirty that Lexy would not let

121

Clem undress. He loved going to bed with most of his clothes still on, and wished he could always do so. When the babies were put to bed, Lexy leaned out of the window and tried to breathe. The houses opposite seemed to be crushing in on her and suffocating her. Then along the dim street she saw her father's returning figure. He was walking very slowly, pausing on every step, and from his bent defeated shoulders she knew that something was wrong.

"Mamma – " she cried. "Here's Papa – "

Joshua came slowly into the room and sank down into a rickety chair with his head in his hands.

"The theatre is closed until further notice, on account of the fever," he said heavily. "Almost as in Clem's little jape on the Wiling troupe, is it not?"

The next few days passed like a nightmare. The Mannerings could not afford to move on, as they had not got enough money for the fares. Cecily kept urging her parents to move out into one of the surrounding villages, where it would be healthier, but Joshua insisted that they must stay on in Scanchester, to be at hand, should the theatre manager suddenly decide to re-open his theatre.

As the week wore on their little store of money became less and less. Finally the day came when Seraphina said to Lexy, "My love. I think we must have bones for the dog today."

Lexy's heart sank, for she knew what this meant. Several times before during hard times she had been sent out to the butcher's to ask for bones for the dog, which most butchers would give away for nothing, and these Seraphina would make into a delicious broth. But Lexy could never enjoy it, because the shame of having to ask for them in the shop, where she felt that everyone knew that they did not have a dog, quite spoilt the taste of the soup.

Today Lexy walked slowly along the hot streets, peering through the windows of all the shops, looking for a friendly butcher. The meat in all of them smelt most unpleasant because of the heat, and many of the butchers appeared to be asleep in chairs, with handkerchiefs over their faces. At last she found a stout jovial one and went in. When she asked for bones in a trembling voice he looked quizzically at her.

"Is it a big dog?" he asked.

"No," said Lexy truthfully, and when he gave her a large bundle she ran out of the shop as quickly as she could.

As she climbed the rickety stairs of their lodgings she began to cheer up at the thought of the broth the bones would make, and how pleased her mother would be. But when she entered the room her mother did not even turn to look at her. She was bending over Jamie's basket.

"Lexy!" she said in a stricken voice. "Come here – Look at Jamie. He's very poorly."

With a sick feeling in the pit of her stomach, Lexy leaned over the baby's basket. His face was very red, and his eyes glazed and staring, and he was whimpering in a highly-pitched voice, like a little animal in pain.

"Mamma!" gasped Lexy. "Is it – ?"

"I fear so," said Seraphina brokenly. "Oh, whatever are we to do?"

"But how has he caught it so quickly?"

"There's fever in this house," said Seraphina dully. "I only discovered it today. The landlady has lost three children these last few weeks. That's why she is so distraught, poor soul. Oh, Lexy, what are we to do?"

124

"I'll go for a doctor." Lexy jumped up, but her mother stopped her. "No, child. How would we pay him? We have nothing – nothing – " And Seraphina started to sob. Lexy put her arms round her mother.

"Don't cry, Mamma. Jamie will get better. He's always had such good care. But we mustn't let Cecily and Clem catch it, must we? They must not come into this room. Now Mamma, please think. What is the best thing to do for fever?" Seraphina dried her eyes.

"Let me see," she said. "The doctors usually bleed folk, for almost everything – But Jamie is so tiny – "

"No, Mamma, that's not the thing for him, I know – Oh, if only we could get him some fresh milk!"

When the others returned, Lexy was very firm and would not even allow them into the room. As the evening drew on, Jamie got steadily worse. Lexy and Seraphina watched beside his basket and took it in turns to nurse him and to soothe him. When the fiery sunset began to colour the room with crimson shadows, Seraphina's head began to nod, and she dozed in her chair. Lexy sat with eyes fixed on Jamic's flushed little face and had long conversations with God.

"Dear God," she began, "I don't really know why you should want to take Jamie away from us. He wouldn't be much good to you. He's nothing but a nuisance really, excepting that he's so sweet. But you must have hundreds of nice babies with you since this epidemic. I suppose that bad things, like babies dying, are sent to test us, but really we have had quite a lot happening to us that serves that purpose. So if you'll spare Jamie, I'll never grumble any more – not about long journeys or poor audiences – or not enough to eat. I'll – I'll even go to school again if you want me to – "

But then she realised that she was only trying to bargain with God and that did not seem quite right. "God will provide" – her father always said – And then she remembered something that she had said to Cecily on the subject – About it being lazy to leave it all to God. And then she remembered a saying of Mrs Tollerton's, "God helps those who help themselves – " And very quietly she picked up her bonnet and made for the door. Outside it was so warm that she could not bother to put it on.

To the first person she met in the street she said, "Can you tell me, please, where the nearest doctor lives?"

"Ay – Across the way. But if it's for the fever he won't take more cases."

Nevertheless, Lexy opened the gate bearing the brass plate with "Dr Smythe" engraved upon it and pulled the bell-pull. A housekeeper opened the door and ushered her into a waiting-room without a word. Lexy's heart sank as she saw that it was crowded with people. She sat on a bench and waited and waited in the hot stuffy room, with the picture of Jamie's flushed little face floating in front of her eyes. The talk went on endlessly, in the flat Scanchester brogue, all about the fever, the deaths, and the heat. And then suddenly one sentence made her sit up. It was an elderly and garrulous old man speaking.

" 'Appen you've 'eard of this rich lord who was took last week. Left 'is body to the saw-bones school, 'e did, to be cut up for experimentalising. Now that I call a reet brave thing. I'd not like to think o' my poor old corpse being tampered with by a lot o' students, gone though I might be – "

The gruesomeness of this thought struck Lexy first, and then she listened to the views of everyone else in the waiting-room. How valuable a thing it was for medical men to discover what ailments had killed people. Some of them, especially the women, expressed horror at the idea, others thought it a generous gesture.

"Ay,"said one, "the doctors'll pay a fine fee for a good corpse."

An idea had formed in Lexy's tired brain – An idea that gave her fresh hope. It seemed hours before she was eventually let into the doctor's surgery. It was very clean and bare and smelt of all the medicines in the world. The doctor had a very long grey beard and an extremely old frock coat.

"And what ails you, my child?" he asked Lexy, in some surprise.

Lexy took a deep breath and said very loudly and clearly, "My baby brother's ill of the fever. I know you won't take more fever cases. Also we have no money – " The doctor made a gesture of impatience, but Lexy went on, "But I am not asking you to treat him for nothing, sir – I will make you a bargain. Do you want a corpse for – for experimentalising on – because if you will cure Jamie, when I die I will leave mine to you in my will. I wouldn't mind at all really. Not if you cured Jamie – " She peered up at him hopefully. The doctor looked blankly at her for a moment and then gave a deep shout of laughter. The next moment he was solemn again, and, rising, came and put an arm round Lexy's shoulder.

"It is a very fair bargain. I will trust you to keep it, and our profession will, I am sure, be most grateful. Come show me where your little brother is – "

127

"Oh, thank you, sir!" Lexy caught his hand and kissed it. He picked up a black bag and his top hat and followed her out into the street. She did not go into Jamie's bedroom with him, but sat outside on the stairs with her head buried on her knees. It was a long time before the doctor reappeared, and then he joined Lexy sitting on the stairs. She did not dare to speak, for fear of what she would hear.

"All will be well," he told her gently. "The crisis was passed before I reached him. I have done my best to ease him and I will call again each day until he is better. He has not got it severely, and he is a sturdy little chap, I can see that. And he has a very brave sister."

"You mean – he won't die?"

"No, child. But as soon as he is well, persuade your play-acting father and your beautiful but, I fear, rather senseless mother, to leave this filthy town and give their bairns a chance. You can persuade them, I can see that. You're the one of the family with the grit, that is quite plain." He patted her shoulder and began to descend the stairs. Lexy followed him, saying, "I cannot thank you enough, sir. One little baby must seem very unimportant to you. But he's not to us. I've only just realised since he's been poorly how much we love him. So thank you – thank you – thank you – "

"I shall call tomorrow. Now you must get some sleep, child. And here – " he handed her a little phial, "wash out your mouth with this, and give some to your mother to do the same, and then you will not catch the baby's infection."

As Lexy waved to him from the doorstep there came a soft rustling whisper as the first longed-for drops of rain began to fall. Lexy turned her face up to the sky, and the raindrops mingled with her tears of relief.

CHAPTER 8

Come to the Fair

"Mamma, Papa – " Clem came running excitedly into the dressing-room, "Ive just seen the fair – the Michaelmas fair – It's all down the street – When can we go?"

They had arrived the day before in the large town of Shefferton where they were to play in a small dismal theatre that appeared to have been closed for years before their arrival. It was in a poor quarter of the town, and they had not yet had time to explore the more fashionable parts, but Clem had been taken out for a treat to a pastrycook's by Mrs Tollerton.

"It's splendid, Mamma, the fair is – " Clem babbled on. "There's gingerbread, and a dentist pulling teeth, and a bearded lady and – "

"Hush, Clem. Do not get so excited. We shall not have time for the fair until the end of the week."

"But it may be gone by then," wailed Clem.

"Nonsense," said Joshua, "the Shefferton Michaelmas fair lasts a good week to be sure."

Clem pouted and kicked the toes of his boots against the wall.

"Now do not be such a wicked boy!" scolded

Seraphina. "You have just had a lovely treat with Mrs Tollerton."

"I ate six buns," said Clem, "and had to let out my belt."

"Oh, Clem. You're disgraceful – whatever did Mrs Tollerton say?"

"She let out her belt too!"

Clem could not forget his glimpse of the fair and continued to talk of it throughout the evening.

"Couldn't we go there tomorrow, Lexy?" he pleaded. "Just you and me. And I will buy you some gingerbread. A whole ha'p'orth."

Lexy sighed. It did seem hard that no-one should have time to take Clem to the fair. He had so little of the enjoyments of most children of his age.

"I've still got last week's penny," urged Clem, "and – p'raps Papa would give us next week's a little early – "

"No, don't trouble Papa," Lexy told him. "I'll try to find time to take you to the fair after rehearsal tomorrow. I've got my spending money too, so we won't ask for next week's."

It was very difficult to find time the following day, for there were the usual mountains of work waiting for Lexy. She had some new lines to study, there was a pile of napkins waiting to be washed for Jamie and neither Seraphina nor Cecily showed any signs of doing them, and Cecily had gone on the previous evening in such a crumpled gown that Lexy had felt it was a disgrace to the company and vowed to iron it as soon as she could. But as she was looking round the untidy dressing-room Clem came in with his lower lip sticking out and said:

"I *knew* you were only telling stories – and we're not

131

to go to the fair after all. Nothing nice ever happens. Only nasty things."

Lexy suddenly reached for her cloak.

"Oh yes it does, Clem. We're going to the fair this minute."

She found his cap, shaped like a little Dutch boy's, with a peak, and told him to bring his coat, as the evenings were beginning to draw in.

"Your overall is dirty, but we can't help that," she said. "Now come quickly and don't tell anyone where we're going."

They sauntered to the stage-door, meeting no-one but Barney Fidgett who was complaining at the lack of any sort of green-room or artistes' refreshment bar in this theatre.

"Yes, Mr Fidgett. We're going out for a bite now," said Lexy innocently.

"That's all – " added Clem unnecessarily.

There was a definite tang of autumn as they stepped outside the stage door, and some dead leaves blew down the dark alleyway that led to the street.

"Isn't it 'citing, Lexy," whispered Clem, scampering along at her side.

"We can only stay a little while," Lexy warned him, "and you're not to make scenes when it's time to come back. Now – do you know the way?"

Almost sniffing the air, like a young puppy, Clem led the way.

The Michaelmas fair at Shefferton was a very large one, for not only was it a festive occasion for the townspeople but for the surrounding country folk it was a hiring fair, to which they came to find new posts as dairymen, labourers, milkmaids and domestic servants for the next six months.

As they approached the main street, whence came the sound of music and cries of the booth-keepers, they passed many groups of these country folk in their heavy fustian clothes, clogs and smocks, bargaining with the farmers for employment.

The nearer the children came to the fair, the quicker grew their pace, and as they burst out of a side street that led into the highway they were almost running.

The noise in the High Street was indescribable. A German band mingled its cacophony with the song of a ballad-singer who was peddling long strips of paper bearing the words of his works. The stall-keepers were all bellowing their wares, and an Italian organ-grinder, with his monkey gibbering on his shoulder, churned out a Neapolitan air. There were stalls selling gingerbread and baked chestnuts, and hot negus to drink, there were fortune tellers, freak-shows, "penny gaffs" – the little miniature theatres, where a short show of half an hour or so was enacted and admission cost only one penny. And all amongst the crowds who thronged the street were the performing midgets, the tumblers and the stilt-walkers.

"Oh – " gasped Clem. "Isn't it prime – Look – look – look – " was all he could say. His eyes were enormous, and he could not turn his head quickly enough to take in all that was going on.

And now came the burning question of how they should spend their money. There were so many exciting things to tempt them.

"I *did* promise you some gingerbread," began Clem reluctantly.

133

"Do not fret about that," said Lexy, "for I have twopence, and you only have a penny. Let's spend our money on something more lasting – or something to see – what about the wax-works?"

There was a tent marked "Wax-works", outside which stood a fearsome waxen Highland gentleman, complete with kilt and sporran bearing a notice saying, "Only one halfpenny admission to the grand wax-works show."

"No," argued Clem. "Let's find something more lively."

But they could not come to any agreement. When Lexy suggested going to see the five-legged calf, Clem would have preferred to watch the lady being sawn in two. Eventually Lexy, exasperated, said, "Well, please yourself. I shall spend mine as I wish, and so may you."

At this moment she saw a small crowd of people jostling into a tiny tent bearing a sign that said, "The Happy Family." Outside a barker was nearly bursting his lungs to make himself heard above the dim.

"Step inside, my lords and ladies," he was shouting. "See the happy family of animals – just as foretold in the Scriptures – 'The lion shall lie down with the lamb' – see it happen before your very eyes. See also, my lords and ladies – the birds' village and the two-headed fish. One penny only."

"That sounds fascinating," said Lexy. "Do let us go in."

"No," objected Clem. "Too expensive. No gingerbread."

"Well, *I* shall go in," said Lexy, "and you are to wait

134

for me here. Do not stir from this very spot." She drew him
to a relatively uncrowded space between two booths.

"Mayn't I go and buy my gingerbread?" whined
Clem.

"No," said Lexy. "If you've stirred a step, I shall
take you straight home."

"You're a spoil-sport," said Clem.

"You're an ungrateful good-for-nothing!"

And with these words they parted.

Although the "Happy Family" was very interesting,
Lexy did not feel quite happy at having left Clem outside
amongst all the crowds of merrymakers. She looked hastily
at the large cage in which were a rather sleepy-looking tiger,
an elderly sheep and a mongrel dog, and then turned her
attention to the smaller cage, in which was a large number
of birds of various sorts, canaries, wrens and sparrows, all
rather bedraggled, but all dressed up in most amazing
fashion. There was a model butcher's shop, hung with tiny
wax joints, and behind the counter stood a robin wearing a
striped apron. There was a tiny model church, and when
the showman played a wedding march on a tin whistle, out
through the door hopped a canary with a tiny top hat on its
head, and beside him his bride wearing a white wreath. In
perfect time they hopped down the path to a waiting
carriage into which they fluttered and were drawn off by a
team of tiny wrens. Lexy clapped her hands with delight
and wished that Clem had come inside to see it. She lingered
over the birds far longer than she had intended, indeed until
the showman emptied the tent ready for the next batch of
spectators.

"There now," she thought, as the left the tent, "I

never saw the two-headed fish." And then she stopped stockstill with alarm, for Clem was not there.

"The young limb," she murmured under her breath. He had no doubt gone to a gingerbread stall despite her warnings. But they had passed so many she did not know in which direction to look first.

"He'll come back here, surely – " she thought "I'd best wait."

She waited for a long time, and the evening air became chillier, and the booths were illuminated with naphtha flares – and some with rough torches of wood soaked in paraffin. They threw fantastic shadows over the faces of the merry-makers, who were by now changing from the staid family parties to the riotous gangs of youths and workmen out for a bit of fun and possibly a bit of trouble. Lexy shrank back into the shadows, to keep out of their way, and yet was afraid of obscuring herself too much, in case Clem came back and could not find her. She had no idea what the time could be and was too frightened to ask anybody. At all events they would be late for the evening show, that was quite clear to her.

When he did not return after some long while, she decided to go and look for him. Probably they had taken a liking to him at the stall and were keeping him there, petting him and feeding him up with gingerbread. That would put all thought of the time out of his head. She rehearsed to herself all the cross things she would say to him when she found him. When she reached the first gingerbread stall she spoke to the woman behind it, who wore a shawl round her head and was bundled up with wraps so that she looked like a cottage loaf:

136

"Have you, I wonder, seen a little boy, with – with a peaked cap?"

"Ay – I've seen a-many – " was the reply.

"He's only six – and – I've lost him – "

But the woman was already serving a customer.

Despairingly, Lexy retraced her footsteps and went to the nearest gingerbread stall on the other side of the "Happy Family", keeping her eyes open for Clem all the time. There were all sorts and conditions of little boys – barefooted little urchins with tousled heads, country boys in their smocks, town boys in overalls and clogs, in caps, in hats, in mufflers – but no Clem. When she reached the second gingerbread stall, she repeated her question, adding, "He has long, golden curls to his shoulders."

"Nay – " said the man behind the stall. "Ah've seen nowt o' the sort."

Now Lexy began to get really frightened, and she pushed wildly through the crowds so that people turned to look at her. The fair seemed to stretch down several intersecting streets, and soon she had even lost her way back to the "Happy Family". Nearly in tears, she halted exhausted, and wondered what to do. Close at hand was a letter-writer's stall, where, for a penny, an old, old man would slowly scrawl out whatever letter his customer dictated. This gave Lexy an idea. At least she could stop her parents worrying about their absence.

"Please, will you write a letter for me?"

"Whatever you please, Missy," said the old gentleman kindly, taking up his quill pen and reaching for the ink-bottle and the sand he threw on the writing to dry it.

"Now, Missy, is it to your school-mate, your sweet-heart – your god-parents?"

"To – my parents," faltered Lexy. She had never dictated a letter before, as she had learned to write at an early age, but lacking pen, paper and ink of her own, this seemed to her the best way of sending her parents a message.

"My most respected parents?" suggested the scribe.

Lexy thought that too stilted.

"My *dearest* parents," she said firmly, "Clem and I have gone to the fair. We did not mean to be late. But now Clem is lost, and I cannot return until I find him – "

Suddenly the full meaning of her plight descended on her and she burst into tears. The old man was immediately sympathetic.

"Now, come, don't cry now little missy," he said. "We'll soon find your little brother – wait now while I finish this – dry your eyes on my pocket handkerchief."

He pushed a large grubby rag towards her, but Lexy hastily said, "I have one of my own, thank you."

"Now, how do you wish to sign yourself? – 'Your obedient daughter' – ?"

"No," said Lexy, shamefaced. "They won't think I've been very obedient, I am afraid. How about just, 'With love'?"

He shook his head, "Too light-hearted for the situation. 'With daughterly salutations'?" He cocked his head on one side like an old crow, to see if she liked it.

"Oh, no," said Lexy. "They would not think it was truly I who was writing. I'll just sign it myself in my own hand-writing – that will assure them."

She did so.

138

"And will you address it please, to Joshua Mannering, Royalty Theatre, Shefferton."

The little old man's eyes opened wide. "Play-actors, eh? Now I was with a troupe once when I was a young, handsome fellow. That's how I got my education. All the Romeos I used to play – " he cackled happily. "My, I was young and tall then, though you'll never believe it."

"Oh, I do believe it," said Lexy earnestly. "I could see you weren't just an ordinary person. You're much too kind and understanding. Now, I must see to getting this delivered – "

She turned to a dirty little boy who was strolling by, licking at a toffee apple.

"If you'll deliver this note to the Royalty Theatre, a gentleman there will give you a penny."

The little boy looked at her with calculating eyes that reminded her of Clem's.

"Truly! See, I'll write it on the envelope."

She hastily scrawled on it, "Give the bearer a penny, please Papa."

The urchin looked at it blankly.

"Can't read," he said, and made no move to go.

"Oh, deary me – " Lexy sighed, "I'd give you *my* last penny, but I owe it to the letter-writer here."

The little old man suddenly thrust out a skinny hand into her face. She gave him the penny, and he turned to the urchin, "Catch, young fellow-me-lad – let that speed you – " and he tossed the penny to him.

It was caught in a flash, and the small messenger was gone with the letter all in one movement.

"That *was* kind of you," said Lexy, feeling a little

139

happier now that she had found a friend. "But what's to be done now?"

The old man started to put his things together.

"I'll come round with you, Missy. I know most of the stall-holders. They'll listen to me."

"Oh, no," said Lexy. "You mustn't shut up your stall – "

"It's no matter," said he. "There won't be many more letters written tonight, I can see. It's more the time for drinking and racketing by now."

All his equipment went into a little bundle on his back, which he told Lexy contained all that he needed in the world.

"Come now," he said, and taking Lexy by the hand began to lead her through the thronging crowds. Every now and then he would leave her side to go and enquire from the stall-keepers, the barkers at the side-shows and the peddlers of everything under the sun, whether or not they had seen a little boy such as Lexy had described to him. Above the babel of the fair, Lexy saw them look a little interested, turn to glance at her as the old man mentioned her and then shake their heads and turn back to their work.

"Do you think it will be of any use?" she enquired in a small voice, after a while.

"Take heart," he said comfortingly. "It's darkest before the dawn, as they say. The young man can only have strayed and lost himself in the crowds. Now, stay; I'll ask my friend here."

He stopped at a stall selling apples, behind which was a large lady with rosy-apple cheeks. Once again Lexy watched the pantomime of question and answer. At first the woman shook her head. Then the old man seemed to add something about Clem's long curls, for he waved his hands about his shoulders and the woman's eyes livened, and she nodded vigorously.

"Missy, Missy!" shouted the old man. "Here's news – "

Lexy pushed close to the stall, but still could not hear what the woman was saying.

"She says she saw a child in a peaked cap and with long golden curls, walking along with a rough, darkish-looking man in working clothes, and wondered at the man having such a superior-looking child."

"That must be Clem – Oh, which way did he go? Do you think it's a gipsy that has stolen him?"

The woman shook her head and said something, but still Lexy could not hear above the noise. The old man thanked her profusely, and as they left the stall she tossed an apple to Lexy and seemed to be calling out good wishes to them.

"They were going in this direction, she said." He led her towards the fringe of the fair, where it seemed to become very dark and still quite suddenly after the crowds and flaring lights. Here there were a lot of horses tethered, and wagons and traps, and all the varying vehicles in which people had come to the fair. There were several ragged boys tending the horses, and to one of these the letter-writer said, "Have ye seen a darkish, working fellow with a little fair curly-haired boy at all?"

"Nay – " came the drawled reply, with much head-shaking. Then suddenly another voice out of the darkness.

"Ay, I seen un – in a pony-trap."

"In a trap?" repeated Lexy.

"Ay, and went off along the Chuffham road." He pointed away into the darkness.

"And – the little boy with him?" gasped Lexy.

"Ay – the both together."

"Oh, thank you," said Lexy tremulously and gave the boy her apple which she had not had the heart to eat.

He munched it gratefully, as if he had not had a meal for days. She turned to the old man.

"Gone – In a pony-trap – " Her heart sank so heavily that she felt quite sick. "Now we shall never find him. But why should the man take him away?"

The old man was shaking his head gravely.

"If only we might follow them – " he said. "Your father has got no horses, I suppose?" he continued hopefully.

Lexy shook her head.

"Only the funny ones we use for the burlesque, but they have to have two men inside to make them move."

Suddenly the little old man disappeared into the darkness, shouting back over his shoulder, "Wait for me there."

For the second time that evening Lexy just stood and waited. By now she was freezing cold and shivering with fear and unhappiness. Every minute's delay seemed to add to Clem's danger. Soon there was a sound of hooves on the cobbles and turning round Lexy saw to her amazement that the letter-writer had returned leading an old lame bony nag that surveyed Lexy with mournful eyes and shook its head from side to side despairingly.

"Where *did* you get that?" cried Lexy.

"I've borrowed him from the applewoman," was the

reply. "She rides to market on him, but will not need him tonight as she's to stay in the town."

"And – and are you going to ride that?" said Lexy.

"We both shall."

The old man scrambled up on to the pony's back and made room for Lexy behind him.

"I don't know how to ride – " wailed Lexy.

"Just hold on to me," said the letter-writer, "and you'll do finely."

He reached down and hoisted her up behind him. The ragged boys laughed loudly as the two of them, clinging on to the nag's back, slowly moved off, clip-clopping down the road.

The pony was very thin and so was Lexy, and the result was extremely uncomfortable. The little old man was very bony too, and Lexy had to hold tight to him to stop herself from falling off altogether. Lexy felt that she was as uncomfortable as it was possible for a human to be. But if only they might find Clem it would all be worth it. At every turning the man kept dismounting and asking people if they had seen a man and a boy in a pony-trap. Several times they received direct assurance that they had passed only a short while before, and this gave Lexy fresh hope.

"We'll not overtake them, it's clear," said the man, "but like as not we'll follow them to where they're bound."

"Ye – ye – yes," said Lexy, bumping up and down behind him.

They seemed to go bouncing along all night. In spite of the discomfort, Lexy was so tired that her eyes kept closing and she would begin to sway over to one side of the pony. Then a particularly rough piece of road or an owl screeching overhead would wake her up with a jerk. The

143

whole situation did not seem real to her now. Why she should be clinging round the waist of a travelling letter-writer on an ancient nag right out on a country road miles from anywhere, when she should be safely in the theatre in the middle of the evening show, she could not understand. And what her parents must be going through she dared not think.

Above them there was a moon that seemed to be riding across the sky in the opposite direction on a steed of clouds and it made her quite giddy to look at it. The letter-writer was singing little songs to try and cheer them up, and urging her to join the chorus, but as each chorus seemed different from the last it was rather difficult. And then, far ahead along the road they saw a little light moving steadily along.

"I wonder – " said the letter-writer, "is that the lamp on a trap?"

Lexy strained her eyes but still it only seemed like a little star dancing along the roads in front of them. The old man stopped the nag, and they listened – yes, there in the distance was the tiny sound of hooves and a faint rattle of wheels.

"That'll be him – the blackguard!" cried the old man and whipped up the nag.

"Please, God," prayed Lexy bumpily, "let that be Clem and let us catch them up."

It really seemed as if they might. The poor old pony responded nobly to the urging and rattled along for all he was worth, but then a delay occurred in the shape of a toll-gate. This was a barrier across the highway where a man living in a little house right beside the road demanded a small fee before allowing them to pass. The letter-writer had to dismount and undo his bundle in order to find his money, and as he did so the turnpike looked at Lexy suspiciously.

"Reckon this bain't your darter," he observed.

"Your reckonings are correct," said the letter-writer.

"Nor neither your grand-darter – "

"Neither, my friend."

"Then what be her name?"

The letter-writer scratched his head.

"I cannot tell 'ee – for I've not asked her."

"My name is Alexandra Mannering – And this is – a friend of mine."

"Do you know *his* name, by any chance?"

"No, I only know he is a letter-writer."

"Ay – I know you, my man. Bartholomew, the Scribe, they call you – And what might you be doing riding off with a well-spoken young girl the likes of this? To hold her up for ransom from her sorrowing parents, I'll be bound." The turnkpike loomed threateningly over the letter-writer.

"No, no, no – " Lexy interrupted. "You are

145

mistaken I assure you, for it's not this man who is carrying *me* off for ransom; it is my little brother, Clem. Did he pass here a while ago – a little boy with long fair curls, and a – a dark, rough-looking man in a pony-trap?"

The turnpike rubbed his chin. "Ay – there was a trap with a man and a child, all wrapped up in a blanket – but I didn't notice if it was boy or girl."

Lexy was relieved to hear that Clem was at least snugly wrapped up.

"Well," she explained, "*they* are the ones you should have stopped and questioned. Now, please let us continue on our way for we shall never overtake them now."

"Yes," said Bartholomew, the letter-writer, "and save your questionings for the right people and stop delaying honest folks."

He tried to scramble up on the pony with dignity, but nearly fell over the other side. Lexy could not help laughing a little hysterically. The situation was so funny – the turnpike thinking that Bartholomew had kidnapped her and stopping them in their pursuit of Clem and his captor.

And then they were off again, jogging along the roads; but the lamp on the pony-trap ahead of them had completely disappeared. Lexy dozed fitfully, until suddenly an enormous jolt woke her and she sat up to find herself sitting in the middle of the road and Bartholomew bending over her.

"Are you hurt, Missy?" he said anxiously.

"No, not a bit," she said. "Whatever has happened?"

"The nag has gone lame – he slipped and threw you – poor beast. He's in no shape for a journey like this. We can't drive him further tonight."

"Oh dear!" sighed Lexy. "What are we to do then?"

"As fortune would have it, we are near to a farm."
He indicated a straggling line of buildings on one side of
the road. "I dare not wake them at this hour of the night,
but we may find some shelter in a barn or an out-house."
He lifted the latch of the gate and immediately dogs started
to bark from the farmyard. But they appeared to be chained
up, and no sign of life came from the house. Bartholomew
stepped inside and disappeared into the darkness. Within a
few minutes he was back.

"There's just the place – " he whispered, "a barn
full of the sweetest hay – better than a feather bed, I tell
you. Step softly, now."

With the old pony limping along behind them they
picked their way across the yard and into the barn. It was
pitch dark, but the hay smelt sweet and felt as soft as down.
With sighs of relief Lexy sank into it, while Bartholomew
tied up the pony before settling down himself. Lexy knew
that she should be worried about Clem and about her
parents, but she was so exhausted that she just let sleep
envelop her like a fleecy cloud.

When she awoke sunlight was flooding into the barn,
and a large sheep-dog was standing looking suspiciously at
them. He backed away and began to bark when Lexy held
out her hand and said, "Good dog then". Immediately a
big man in a smock appeared behind the dog and also
looked suspiciously at them. Lexy thought it best to start
explaining their presence.

"Good morning," she said. "My name is Alexandra
Mannering. My little brother has been stolen and we are
looking for him. This is Bartholomew, the Scribe, as they
call him. And this the applewoman's pony which we
borrowed to take us to look for Clem."

147

Bartholomew began to wake, with a lot of groaning and grunting and stretching. He greeted the farmer and they appeared to know each other slightly. Bartholomew asked if they might wash under the pump in the yard, and the farmer answered gruffly, "Ay, and take a bite in the kitchen with the missus and me."

Lexy was delighted, for she was feeling distinctly empty inside, having had no supper the evening before, and also very uncomfortable and untidy from having slept in all her clothes.

As she splashed her face under the pump, with Bartholomew working the handle for her, all the happenings of the previous day came back to her and she thought of how worried her parents must be. But in the long stone-flagged farm kitchen there was set out a fine breakfast of eggs and home-cured ham, and porridge and new bread and farm butter and delicious preserves. The farmer and his wife and the farm hands all sat down together, and there was little conversation because they were all so busy eating. When at last she could eat no more Lexy leaned back in her chair and said to the farmer, "I suppose you've no idea who this man might be that has stolen away my brother? He must live in these parts as he was at the Shefferton fair."

The farmer shook his head. "Folk come to the Shefferton fair from miles around," he observed. "It's hard to tell who he might be – "

"D'you think it was a gipsy?" asked Lexy fearfully

"It'll never be a gipsy," said the farmer's wife, "not in a pony and trap – p'raps it's a farmer as wants a strong lad."

"But Clem *isn't* strong. He's tiny, and no good at

anything but acting. Papa always joked and said if anyone stole Clem they'd bring him back again."

She blinked away tears to think that they had once joked happily about the subject.

Bartholomew seemed disposed to linger over his breakfast, but Lexy said to him, "Hadn't we best see how the pony is feeling this morning, and whether he can go any farther?"

The farmer came and looked at the pony too, and gave him some oats, and after his breakfast he seemed to feel better and did not appear to be lame.

"Ah, he'll carry you a mile or two farther," said the farmer.

They said goodbye with many thanks for the hospitality. Bartholomew had tried to press some payment upon the farmer but had been told that they were only too pleased to welcome travellers.

"Isn't it strange how different country folk are from townsfolk? Compare that farmer to all the landladies of lodgings in the towns, who almost charge you for the air you breathe," Lexy said.

"Folk that live amongst God's good gifts can afford to be generous," observed Bartholomew wisely, as he helped Lexy up on to the pony again. She was so stiff from her long ride the previous day that she almost suggested that she should walk alongside, but she knew that speed was important in their search for Clem.

A few miles down the road they stopped outside an inn, "The Load of Hay", and leaving Lexy outside, Bartholomew went in to make some enquiries. He reappeared a few minutes later, capering with joy –

"Here's news, my little lady, good news. They stayed

here the night, the pair o' them – he told me the man's name and all – the landlord did – 'tis Joe Briggs, the chimney-sweep from a village called Chuffham, some miles along the road."

Lexy's face had blanched, and she felt her stomach turn over with fear.

"A *chimney-sweep*," she breathed. "Oh, how terrible. So *that's* what he wants with Clem."

It was very often the case that in order to sweep the enormous broad chimneys of the houses and factories a sweep would use a small boy who could climb up inside the chimney, clearing out the soot as he went. It was hard, dangerous work and bad for the lungs and the eyes. For a long time there had been public feeling against it, but as no law had yet been passed, it was still going on, and small active boys were very valuable to a chimney-sweep. At the thought of Clem climbing up a dark, sooty chimney, Lexy was nearly distraught.

"Bartholomew!" she cried. "Oh, we must find him before that cruel man makes him climb up any chimneys. Poor little mite – it will kill him."

Bartholomew too was beginning to look serious, now that he had got over his joy at the success of his detective work. He mounted the pony again.

"Ay, we'll find him, and I'll give the scoundrel the rough side of my tongue for carrying off a child like that from his family. He could be sent to jail for life for that, and I don't doubt that's what your Papa will see done to him."

"Oh, no!" said Lexy hurriedly. "I don't care for sending him to jail. And let us have no upsets when we find

150

him. Let us just pick Clem up and hurry away. We don't want any fighting or such – "

"But do you think he'll give him up without a fight?" demanded Bartholomew grimly. "A young slip of a boy like your brother is a sweep's livelihood."

"He *must* give him back when he sees that I am his sister and have come to find him. Oh, I wish we were there already. How far is it?"

"Another ten miles. Country miles, I fear. But take heart now, little miss, we shall soon find your brother."

On they went over the moorland intersected by rough walls of white stone, with only occasionally a labourer's little cottage. Bartholomew talked to Lexy to try and distract her mind and asked her all about the troupe and what plays they did, and what parts she took in them. Then he sighed heartily.

"Ah, it's like music in my ears – to hear about the boards again. It's nigh on fifty years since I was a play-actor, but I still go over the lines of my favourite parts in my head before I go to sleep. It's a fine life. A fine life."

"But writing letters must be very interesting too," said Lexy. "You must meet all sorts of people and learn all about them."

Bartholomew shook his head.

"Too much. Too much. They do not write the truth. 'Dearest mother', they write, 'I cannot send you money this week for I am starving myself – ' and there they are in silks and satins. Or 'My fond sweetheart', they write, 'I pine for you night and day' and there is another wench on their arm as I write it for them – No, I prefer a world of make-believe behind the footlights."

"Look ahead," cried Lexy suddenly. "Is not that a

large village or a small town in the valley? Could that be Chuffham?"

"It could, please God," said Bartholomew reverently.

They seemed to take hours to get near to the village. Lexy looked anxiously at the smoke coming out of the chimneys and wondered in which of those that had no smoke poor Clem might be clinging and scrambling.

"We'll ask as soon as we see someone," said Bartholomew.

But the first person they met seemed to be the village idiot, for he just gaped at their questions and said, "Maybe – Maybe not," to everything they asked. The next person they met was a little girl, who stared curiously at them. When Bartholomew asked where Joe Briggs, the sweep, lived she replied, "Near the blacksmith's' and walked on. The next passer-by was a very garrulous old man, who insisted on telling them that he remembered Joe Briggs as a babe in arms. "Ay, and his father afore him."

"Don't let us trouble to ask then," urged Lexy, "for he's sure to have a sign out."

So they proceeded along the main street, followed by the inquisitive glances of the inhabitants.

There seemed to be signs out for every other trade – bakers, blacksmiths, chandlers, but no chimney-sweep. Soon they were on the outskirts of the far side of the village without any success.

"I'll go by myself on foot," said Lexy, clambering down, and quite glad to be on her feet for a bit. "You rest here a while."

Bartholomew was a bit wary of letting her go off by herself, but Lexy felt sure that they must have missed the side street in which Joe Briggs lived. Meeting a middle-aged woman she enquired of her where Joe Briggs, the sweep, lived.

"In cottage by canal – " was the answer.

"Which direction is the canal, please?"

The woman looked even more surprised.

"You don't know where canal is? Everybody knows where canal is – " She seemsd quite upset at Lexy's ignorance.

"I do not. I'm a stranger here."

"Ay, I can see that," said the woman. "Well, you turn down by the pump and follow your nose, turning toward the church, and then when you pass Tucker's mill there it is – you can't miss it."

Lexy was sure that she could, but nevertheless thanked the woman and continued in the direction in which she had pointed. Then she saw a gleam of water that turned out to be a canal, and beside it a huddle of tumble-down cottages, as dirty as any slum in a town, incongruous beside the freshness of the water and the greenness of the tree-lined village streets. Outside the dirtiest cottage was a small notice: "Briggs, Sweep."

Some ragged children were playing and tumbling in the yard, like a litter of puppies. One of them threw a stone at Lexy as she approached. The door had no knocker or bell-pull so she rapped with her knuckles and a slatternly woman came to the door.

"Is Mr Briggs at home – "

"No, 'e's not," she snapped. "E's out working – and so 'e should be, arriving back from the fair at gracious knows how late this morning. What's your business with 'im? What's the address and 'ow many?"

153

Lexy gaped, then realised what she meant.

"Oh, it's not about chimneys – at least it is, in a way – Do you know – Can you tell me – Did Mr Briggs bring a little boy back from the fair with him?" Lexy scanned her face eagerly. A curious look came into the woman's eyes –

"What would 'e be wanting with a little boy – Can't you see we've got a-plenty?"

The ragged children were peeping round a corner of the wall. Lexy looked at the woman levelly, "They're too young," she said, "aren't they?"

The woman suddenly became flustered and shut the door in her face. Lexy walked away, sunk in thought. It was quite clear that this was the right place. Mr Briggs was certainly the sweep who had stolen Clem, and if she waited long enough he would surely bring him back to the cottage. But she must find them before Clem was exposed to the perils of his new occupation.

Once again she started making fruitless enquiries. But everyone of whom she enquired if they had seen Joe Briggs, either could not understand her way of speaking or was too suspicious of her to answer. Eventually, at a complete loss, she found herself back where she had left Bartholomew and the pony. To her surprise Bartholomew was waving and gesticulating wildly.

"Thank heaven you've returned," he said. "Just after you went a carter passed by, and I enquired for Joe Briggs, thinking it would do no harm and he replied, 'Joe Briggs, why, you'll find him up at the Grange doing the chimneys.' I asked where the Grange might be, and 'tis that tall house set back from the road that we passed before coming into the village. Quickly, now, there is no time to lose."

"I found his house," gasped Lexy, as they bumped

along again, "and I saw his wife, I think, but she wouldn't say anything about Clem, so that must mean that he *has* got him, mustn't it?"

"Without a doubt. And the carter said he had a young lad with him – But I asked did he have long fair curls, and he said no – "

"Perhaps it isn't him – " said Lexy alarmed. "Or, perhaps – perhaps they've cut off his beautiful curls – Oh, whatever will Mamma and Papa say? They are so valuable to him on the stage."

"They'd get dirty in a flue," observed Bartholomew. "Doubtless they've cut them off and sold them – "

"Oh, no – " cried Lexy. "Oh, Bartholomew," she cried, "do hurry."

The old nag staggered along, almost as if he knew that the goal of his journey was in sight.

"There it is – " cried Bartholomew, as they rounded a bend in the road. The Grange was a large house set back from the road, with a drive leading up to it. There was no smoke coming out of any of the chimneys and Lexy scanned them anxiously for some sign that they were being swept, but there was none.

"We'd best go round the back door," said Bartholomew, as they reached the imposing façade of the house.

When Bartholomew reined in their faithful steed, Lexy slid off his back and ran and knocked at the door. It was opened by a very smart parlour-maid in a frilly cap and apron. She took one look at Lexy and then at Bartholomew standing with his bundle on his back, holding the pony's head, and said, "Not today, thank you." The door was shut before Lexy could say a word.

Bartholomew's lined face screwed itself up into a

smile, "She thought we were peddlers or tinkers, I'll be bound."

Lexy looked down at her crumpled clothes and pulled a few odd pieces of hay from the barn out of her hair. She realised that she must look like a vagabond child, and it was no wonder that doors were shut in her face. But she had got to get inside the Grange to find Clem. Bracing her courage she knocked at the door again. This time a burly footman opened it and raised his arm threateningly.

"Be off, you young varmint. We've told you we need nothing."

Quickly Lexy dodged under the raised arm, through the scullery, through the kitchen where the staff were just sitting down to a well-laden table, and out into a passage. There were immediate cries of "Stop, thief!" and "Catch her!" and she heard the sound of several pairs of pursuing feet. She looked in at every open door that she passed but there was no sign of a chimney-sweep. In several of the rooms furniture was covered with dust sheets, and this gave Lexy hope. None of the rooms seemed to be inhabited, the only sign of life being in the servants' quarters. The footsteps seemed to be gaining on her, so she slipped into the door of a large linen-cupboard and heard her pursuers pounding past.

When the noise had all died away she crept out again, and tip-toed along the shadowy corridors. The walls were lined with huge oil-paintings in heavy gilt frames, and the carpets were so thick that she seemed to sink into them up to her ankles. She mounted flight after flight of stairs, peering into all the rooms on every landing. The servants seemed to have returned to their quarters by another staircase.

And then Lexy began to smell soot. It was quite a different smell from the mustiness of most of the rooms and

corridors. It was definitely soot – freshly-disturbed soot. She
sniffed along the passage, and then she heard the sound of
movement in one of the rooms. Bending down she looked
through the large keyhole. All the furniture was shrouded
in dust sheets, and a man with a blackened face was kneeling
on the hearth. There was soot everywhere, and some of it
floating through the keyhole nearly made Lexy choke. As
she watched, the sweep put his head up the chimney and
shouted, "Come on up there, you rascal, or I'll light a fire
to warm you up a little – "

Lexy almost shouted with anger, and went to turn
the door-knob and enter, but then she was afraid. He was
such a big man and seemed so fierce. Instead, she turned
and made for a narrow winding staircase that seemed to go
up to the roof. There was a small door at the top of it that
gave out on to the leads and the eaves of the attics rose
above them. It was a forest of attic roofs and chimney
stacks. Lexy could hardly believe that they all belonged to
one house. An attic window looked out on to this part of
the roof, and, combing her hair at a mirror in the window
stood the smart parlour-maid who had opened the back
door. When she saw Lexy she screamed and hurried away
from the window. Lexy could hear her shouting to the rest
of the household that the gipsy child was on the roof. She
knew that she had not much time to lose. Looking over the
edge of the roof to the ground below she became quite
dizzy, and was afraid that she would fall. Then she mustered
all her strength and shouted at the top of her voice, "Clem
– Clem, where are you?"

It seemed to her that she heard a muffled reply, but
she could not be sure. From below came a shout from
Bartholomew. "Alexandra! Are you safe?"

"Yes, Bartholomew," she shouted back. "I've nearly found him."

In the distance she could hear the noise of the servants in pursuit of her once more.

"What's to do, young varmint?" came a hoarse voice from below.

Lexy ran wildly over the roof-top on the narrow strips of lead, between the tent-like structures of the attic roofs.

"Clem," she shouted, "it's Lexy. I've come to rescue you – "

Suddenly out from the top of one of the biggest chimneys popped a little head. It was coal-black, like a miner's – black, sooty curls, black face, big shining blue eyes, and an expanse of white teeth. It waved to Lexy, who was so overcome by emotion that she felt quite faint.

"Hullo, Lexy," said Clem. "I don't want rescuing. I *like* being a chimney-sweep."

CHAPTER 9

Little Boy Lost

When Lexy had left Clem standing outside the "Happy Family" tent he had shifted from one foot to the other restlessly, turning over his penny in his pocket and wishing that she would hurry back so that he could go and buy some gingerbread. She seemed to have been gone a very long time, and he began to be afraid that the gingerbread stall would be sold out before he could get there.

"Rotten old Lexy," he thought angrily.

Just then a large man in very shabby clothes, whose face and hands were a strangely grey colour, came up to him and stood looking very hard at him.

"Stare, stare, like a bear, then you'll know me anywhere – " said Clem rudely.

The man did not stir a muscle. Then, in a very deep and rumbly voice, he said, "What be tha' name?"

"You shouldn't say what *be* you should say what *is*," Clem corrected him.

"Ay, but what be it?"

"It be Clem." He experimented with the different styles of grammar. "Clemence Horatio Mannering."

"And where be Papa and Mamma?"

"They're dead," said Clem, without flickering an eyelid. "I've only got a big sister. And she's cruel to me."

The man continued to stare at him speculatively.

"Yes," continued Clem, "she's gone off gallivanting on her own now, and told me not to move from this spot." His big blue eyes filled with tears of self-pity. "And it's *so* cold, and I *do* want some gingerbread."

"Gingerbread, eh? You come along o' me, and I'll find ye some gingerbread."

The man held out a grimy hand.

Clem hesitated. He had been warned never to speak to strangers, but really Lexy was being an uncommonly long time – He put up his hand and immediately it was taken in a vice-like grip, and he was hurried along through the crowd at a tremendous rate.

"There's a gingerbread stall!" he panted as they hurried past one.

"Ay, but there's better further on."

This happened several times, until eventually they found themselves on the fringe of the fair. The man led him to a pony and trap tethered to a post.

"Is this yours?" asked Clem.

"Ay, d'you want a ride?"

"Oh, yes, please," said Clem eagerly, gingerbread forgotten for the moment.

The man helped him up into the trap, cracked his whip threateningly at some of the ragged boys who advanced hoping for a copper for looking after the pony, and then off they went.

"What a splendid little pony!" said Clem as they sped along the road.

The man said nothing. When they had been going

along for some time Clem said, "Hadn't we better turn back now?"

"Not turning back tonight," said the man.

"Not turning back? But – but my sister is waiting for me – "

"If she's a cruel sister, why don't you forget about her and come along o' me?"

"Well, she's not as cruel as all that," said Clem cautiously. "And what would I do along of you?"

"Earn your living like a grown man."

"Oh, but I do already," said Clem. "I'm an actor, you know, and I get a penny a week pocket-money."

"I'd give ye twopence."

Clem worked out how much gingerbread he could buy with that and said promptly, "Yes, I will then. But what do I have to do?"

"D'you care for climbing?"

"Trees?"

"Well, it's very like."

"Oh, yes," said Clem, "I love it. But how can I make a living climbing trees?"

"Not trees, my beauty – flues – "

"Flues?"

"Ay, the chimneys – And sweeping 'em free of soot."

Clem's eyes grew enormously round. "O – oh – You're a chimney-sweep. And I'm to sweep chimneys too?"

"That you are. And we'll make you into a fine sweep, too – "

"Will I have a black face?"

"That you will."

"And never have to wash, ever?"

"Not if you're not so inclined."

"Prime – " said Clem. "And ride about in the pony-trap all the time?"

"Every day."

Clem clapped his hands delightedly.

"Here, you'd best put these wraps round you – " Some very dirty pieces of blanket were flung over him, and he curled up on the hard seat and watched the dark hedges go by. This was much more fun than doing the silly old show. And it would teach Lexy a lesson for leaving him alone like that. Soon he began to doze, and the chimney-sweep put his arm round him to stop him from falling off the narrow seat.

They seemed to drive and drive for hours, and then Clem was just conscious of being lifted down from the trap and carried inside somewhere, where it was warm and there was the sound of clinking glasses. He was carried up some stairs and laid on a bed as he was, and with a noise like a sleepy puppy he just curled up and slept and slept.

When he woke up he found himself in an attic bedroom lying on a bed fully dressed, and in the other bed lay the chimney-sweep, clad in his shirt, snoring with his mouth open. Clem was terribly hungry and suddenly thought of his mother and father. He got up and crossed to the other bed.

"Mr Chimney-sweep," he said loudly, digging him in the ribs at the same time to try and wake him, "I've decided to go home."

The sweep grunted and groaned and turned over. Clem nudged him harder, and the sweep woke up and cursed him.

"I've decided," said Clem firmly, "to go home, if you don't mind."

The sweep took no notice of him, but rolled out of bed and started to pull his clothes on.

"I'm late," he grumbled, "and there's a job to do at the Grange. My brushes be at home, so put your best foot foremost, my man."

"But I'm just telling you," Clem persisted, "I've decided to go home."

In answer the sweep took hold of him by the scruff of the neck and pushed him down the narrow stairs in front of him.

In the bar parlour they hastily gulped down some bread and cheese and cyder as breakfast and went outside to the trap. The sweep drove at a furious pace for some miles, and then when they came to a village turned down a side street to the grimy cottage beside the canal.

"Is this where you live?" demanded Clem.

"Ay."

"Not very nice, is it?"

"It'll do for me. And it'll have to do for you now, my young gentleman. Stir your stumps."

Clem got out of the trap and looked at the dirty children who had come running to the gate.

"Are these yours?" asked Clem.

"Ay, the lot of 'em."

"Dirty, aren't they?" observed Clem. "Shall I be allowed to get as dirty as that?"

The children gathered round him, laughing at his curls and his neat garments.

Clem made the ugliest face that he could think of, and they stopped and looked admiringly at him.

"Come on, young chap," said the sweep.

Clem followed him into the house. In the kitchen a woman was stirring something over an open fire.

"What's this, hey?" she asked, looking at Clem in surprise.

"New apprentice," said the man shortly.

"Another mouth to feed," said the woman.

"He'll work for it."

Clem began to think that he did not much care for his new home. His mother was so much prettier than this mother, and his father so much kinder – The sweep was collecting some long black bristly brushes from an outhouse.

"You're late for the Grange," shouted his wife.

"Overslept."

"Sluggard!" she shouted angrily.

"Aren't you a cross lady?" observed Clem.

She rapped his knuckles with her wooden spoon and told him not to be "imperent".

"It's not 'imperent'," said Clem scornfully. "It's impudent – imp*ud*ent, see?"

The woman shouted out to her husband to come and take this young limb out of her sight before she throttled him.

Joe Briggs bundled Clem into the trap again, ordering him to push all his curls under his cap, and they set off back along the road by which they had entered the village.

"Now, mind y'r quiet and well-behaved at the Grange," the sweep told him. "They're my best customers. Quality. So no snivelling when it comes to going up the flues, or you'll hear from me afterwards."

"I really think I ought to be going home – "

murmured Clem. "Mamma will be – I mean my sister will be – "

"She'll've forgotten ye – " the sweep growled. "Now shut your mouth and save yer breath – ye'll need it later on."

Clem was very impressed by the tree-lined drive that led to the Grange, but was a bit disappointed when they went round to the back door. The be-frilled parlour-maid stuck her nose in the air when she saw them and told Briggs not to mess the place up any more than he could help. The other servants in the servants' hall all thought Clem "a little angel" and the cook gave him some raisins to eat, and they would have kept him there petting him, had not Briggs growled and pulled him away by the ear.

They walked through the long carpeted corridors and then went into a room where the furniture was shrouded with dust sheets. Briggs settled down by the hearth and began to unpack his brushes.

"Well," said Clem, edging towards the door, "I'll be going home now, I think."

The vice-like grip descended on his ear once more.

"Oho, no you don't, my beauty. This is where your day's work begins. And very late in the day it is, too. Most mornings we'll be started by five o'clock."

"Five o'clock!" cried Clem. "But I don't care to get up that early – "

" 'Tis not what *you* care – Now, off with that monkey-jacket and up the flue with you."

Rather slowly Clem took off his coat and cap and went and stood in the broad fireplace, looking upwards. The flue was quite wide, and there were rungs let into the side to provide a foothold. Far away at the top was a patch of blue sky.

165

"What do I do when I get to the top?" he enquired.

"Come down again."

"How silly," said Clem. "I'd like to get out on to the roof and look around."

Briggs gave him a little brush and told him to sweep as he went, and also tied a rope round his waist. In the middle of the length of rope was tied a large bundle of twigs.

"Now when you're at the top, pull the rope up after ye, so that the twigs clean the sides of the flue, and then I pull it back, and so we go on till 'tis clean. Now let's see you shin up there, my young monkey."

Clem found the ascent more difficult than he had visualised. The soot that he disturbed fell into his eyes and mouth and nearly choked him, and he kept scraping his knees against the iron rungs. Some of them were so far apart that he could scarcely reach them. From below, Briggs kept up a constant flow of bullying encouragement. Clem, out of breath, with tears streaming from his eyes, made hurriedly for the opening at the top of the flue. It was very dark and very frightening, and yet he was rather enjoying it. But the thought of all the other chimneys in the house rather depressed him. Some of them joined on to this flue and seemed even darker and dirtier than this one. At last he was within reach of the top – one last haul, and then panting and triumphant he was at the top, perched on the rim of the chimney, at a dizzy height, where he could breathe and see easily again. He was so relieved that he started to sing a little song to himself.

"No larking about now," came a faint voice from below, accompanied by a sharp tug on the tope that nearly brought him tumbling down again.

"Pull on the rope, young 'un," came the order. He did so, hauling up the bundle of twigs and cleaning the sides of the flue, perched precariously on the chimney top. It was very hard and dangerous work and soon exhausted him.

For the rest of the morning the programme was the same, scaling the dark chimneys, and perching on top of them to haul on the rope. He began to get very tired and his knees were cut and bleeding. He remembered how easy life had been when he had nothing to do but walk on to the stage wearing pretty clothes and recite lines that he had learned by heart. It all seemed a very long time ago now. And then as he climbed what seemed like the hundredth chimney, he fancied that he heard Lexy's voice. He knew it must be merely fancy, for Lexy was miles away, but sure enough when he popped his head out of the top of the chimney, there was Lexy as if by magic standing on the leads below, saying she had come to rescue him. He was delighted to see her but felt that he must not appear unhappy in his new occupation. And after all, it did seem rather grand to be sitting up there like that, on top of the world with such a black face.

"Quickly, quickly," shouted Lexy. "Can you jump down here – it's not far?"

"I'm all tied up," observed Clem.

Lexy scrambled up the sloping chimney stack, clinging on almost by her finger nails, and helped him to unfasten the rope from his middle. The noise of the pursuing servants came closer. Briggs was shouting angrily from below as the bundle of twigs fell down the chimney right on top of him.

Lexy took hold of Clem's black little hand and pulled him along to the attic window from which the parlour-maid had seen her. They hid out of sight of the window while the servants ran across the leads, shouting excitedly at each other. Then they slipped through the door and sped down the corridor to the servants' staircase. To gain the main staircase they had to pass the door of the room where Joe Briggs was working. Just as they passed it, he put his head out and saw them.

"Hi," he shouted angrily.

"I'm going home now," Clem called back over his shoulder. Briggs started in pursuit and began to overtake them. The broad marble bannisters of the staircase gave Lexy an idea. Clem was an ardent bannister-slider. She picked him up and placed him astride, and gave him a little push.

"Slide down," she ordered and flung herself on after him.

The rate at which they sped down the polished surface was greater than that at which Briggs could descend, although they wasted some time picking themselves up off the carpet at the bottom. Out through the large front door they ran, to the amazement of the footmen dozing at the entrance, and round to the side of the house. There was Bartholomew, still waiting patiently with the pony.

"Quick, quick," gasped Lexy. "I've found him."

She bundled Clem on to the pony and scrambled up behind him. Bartholomew dug his heels into the poor creature's sides, and off he ambled.

"Quicker, quicker!" cried Lexy, but the load was too great for the old pony to go at much of a speed. Looking back Lexy could see Briggs, untethering the pony and trap. Soon there came the rattle of wheels behind them.

"Oh, what can we do?" cried Lexy.

They were nearing the main road now, and just as they were about to turn into it they saw approaching from the village a flock of sheep, being driven in the direction of Shefferton.

"Quickly," shouted Lexy. "We must get out in front of them!"

They just managed to get into the main road ahead of the flock, and when Joe Briggs in the trap turned out of the drive, he found a seething mass of sheep separating him from the three on the pony. He whipped up his pony and tried to scatter the sheep, but the shepherd roared angrily and the sheep just ran aimlessly backwards and forwards across the road so that Briggs' pony reared and shied. Clem turned round and laughed loudly, and Briggs shook his fist at them. He followed for a while, and then, finding it quite impossible to overtake the flock, he finally gave up and turned his pony back in the direction of the village.

"Oh, thank goodness," cried Lexy. "Oh, Clem, I thought he was going to steal you back again – " Lexy buried her face in Clem's curls and burst into tears of relief.

"Don't be so soft – " He wriggled away from her.

"But Clem, I thought I'd lost you for ever."

Bartholomew reined in the pony, and they all got off. The poor animal promptly sank to the ground in an attitude of exhaustion.

"So this is the young gentleman?" said Bartholomew.

"I've been sweeping chimneys," Clem announced proudly.

"So we can see," said Lexy crossly, "and a fine chase you've given us. Whatever do you think Mamma and Papa must be feeling? How *could* you go off with that wicked man? Did he force you to?"

"Yes," said Clem blandly. "He said he'd kill me if I didn't. But he was quite nice really, you know. He didn't make me wash, not once, the whole time."

Some time after Clem and Lexy had left the theatre the previous evening, Seraphina noticed that they were not there.

"Where have those children disappeared to?" she asked of Cecily. "I trust they're not playing under the stage. It's filthy in that basement room."

"I don't know, Mamma," yawned Cecily, who was dozing over a novelette instead of polishing her lines for the evening show. "But it's a mercy to be wid of them for a while."

It drew nearer and nearer the time for the curtain to go up, and still there was no sign of them. Cecily's gown was still not ironed, Jamie needed some clean napkins, the prompter was looking for Lexy to see if she would hold the book for the first act, and it was time for Clem to be dressed in his costume as the black page of the Prince of Morocco in "The Merchant of Venice". Fortunately both Lexy and Clem only played pages in this production, so their lateness was not such a very serious matter. Seraphina, becoming more anxious, went enquiring of all the members of the company whether or not they had seen them.

"I saw them a while ago, at the stage-door. They said they were going for a bite to eat," Barney Fidgett told her.

"They must have gone to the pastry-cook's at the other end of the town where Mrs Tollerton took Clem yesterday," surmised Seraphina. "Oh, deary me – and that's where the fair is – they're sure to have gone there – the young rascals."

"If they're late for the curtain," stormed Joshua, "they will find themselves in a peck of trouble. If it were any of my other artistes they would receive notice to leave. As it's my own family I can't do that."

"It's so unlike Lexy," said Seraphina in a worried tone. "She's usually so very punctual."

They held the curtain for five minutes, but then were forced to go on. It was a noisy rabble of an audience, who ate oranges audibly and the popping of ginger-beer bottle corks almost drowned the lines spoken by the actors. But Seraphina and Joshua were too worried to care much. Lexy had never missed a show before, and they knew very well that something must be wrong. As they spoke the lines that they had spoken so many times before that they were second nature, they could see the same thoughts reflected in each other's eyes. Even Cecily began to grow worried, and this had the effect of making her dry continually in her rôle of Nerissa, and she kept having to be prompted, which did not escape the notice of the audience.

"Prompter!" they shouted at the end of the act. "Huzza for the prompter!"

For once Joshua was too preoccupied to be cross with her.

As they were about to leave their dressing-rooms to go on for the last act, the stage-door keeper limped along the passage to them.

"A little ragged boy just brought this note for the Guv'nor. I gave him a penny."

"Many thanks." Joshua undid the note hastily and read it, frowning to see the strange handwriting.

"Is it – " began Seraphina, stretching to see over his shoulder.

"Yes – it's from Lexy – or it claims to be – I don't know – "

"Oh, let me see – " Seraphina snatched it from him. "Why, yes, that is her signature at the bottom, but the rest of the writing is not hers – " She broke off in horror as she read it through. "Oh, Clem – he is lost. My poor lamb – "

"Do not fret," Joshua comforted her. "In all probability he has just strayed amongst the crowd. He knows the name of the theatre, does he not?"

"I don't know," said Seraphina, shaking her head anxiously.

"Yes, Mamma, he does," put in Cecily. "Do you not wemember him saying that it did not *look* vewy woyal?"

Seraphina sighed with relief.

"Yes, of course, I remember. Then someone is sure to bring him back safely, aren't they? We must wait here for him and not return to the lodgings, for he does not know that address, I'll swear. I trust Lexy will not wait about in the cold too long, but will come back here like a sensible girl."

"I expect she is fwightened of a scolding if she comes back without Clem," observed Cecily.

"Come, we must proceed with the piece," said Joshua. "We cannot keep our public waiting – however humble they be."

They went through the rest of the play mechanically, keeping one eye on the wings the whole time, expecting to see two anxious little faces appear, but there were none. The after-piece was a short burlesque in which Seraphina sang and danced and Barney Fidgett and Matthew Tollerton had a mock fencing match. The audience enjoyed this much more than Shakespeare and showed their appreciation by throwing nuts and pieces of orange peel on to the stage. Little did they think that underneath the sequins and spangles that covered Seraphina's trim figure was beating a very worried mother's heart as she smiled and blew kisses, looking no more than Cecily's age. The curtain came down on a roar of applause and Seraphina, panting slightly after the effort of five hours' solid work playing Portia and then skipping about in the burlesque, immediately let the gay smile slip from her face, as she hurried into the wings demanding, "Any news?"

Joshua's face was grave. "None. I think I should go and search for them. There may be trouble at the fair. At this time of night it's likely to become rough. Perhaps they cannot get through the streets. You and Cecily and Baby stay here."

Joshua flung on his cloak and was gone. Cecily and Seraphina sat in the draughty dressing-room on hard benches for what seemed like hours. Jamie slept the sleep of blissful babyhood in his basket, and the rats and mice scampered behind the skirting-boards.

"There's something very eerie about an empty theatre," said Seraphina. "It never seems – well, *really* empty, does it?"

"Oh, hush, Mamma. You'll give me the cweeps. It's bad enough thinking of the ghost of Dwuwy Lane, and such storwies."

They began to look nervously over their shoulders every time a board creaked. To cheer themselves up they started to reminisce about their happier days – Seraphina's, when she was one of the toasts of London, in burlesque; Cecily's, when she was the belle of the ball at the Honourable Poppy Pagett's. Each described to the other in minute detail what she was wearing on every occasion.

"It was more of a *crimson* taffeta really – " Seraphina

was just saying when they heard a soft footfall in the corridor outside. They looked at each other with wide, terrified eyes. Then Cecily picked up her heavy metal make-up box and poised it in the air. Seraphina snatched her umbrella from behind the door as it slowly opened. But it was only Joshua, drawn and weary. He looked round the room, as if to see if Clem and Lexy had returned, then sank into a chair. They did not even trouble to ask what was the news.

"They have disappeared!" he told them heavily. "Completely. The booths are all closed up now, and the streets are nearly deserted. And there is no sign of them."

"But where – *where* can they have gone to?" whispered Seraphina. "And what must we do now?"

"We must call out the police force, I fear," said Joshua.

"Oh, perhaps they are at the lodgings," suggested Cecily, suddenly hopeful again, "for if Lexy found Clem, but too late for the show, she would take him back to the lodgings, and not bwing him here, would she not?"

"Of course," cried Seraphina, jumping up with fresh optimism. "Come, Joshua, they may be in bed quite happily when we return. And you won't scold, now will you?"

Joshua shook his head. They put on their cloaks and hurried through the cold, dark streets to their lodgings, which were better than some and worse than others in which they stayed. The landlady was in bed, but they had a front-door key. Supper was left for them in their sitting-room but they ignored it and hurried through into the children's room. The two little beds were quite empty.

Seraphina sat down and began to cry. Cecily tried unsuccessfully to comfort her, and Joshua paced up and down the room.

"I'll wait until the morning," he decided, "and then go to the police force. It would be of no avail at this time of night – of the morning, I should say, for in Shefferton, I am sure, there is no all-night watch. Now, come, my love. You must go to bed and get some rest."

"Rest!" cried Seraphina. "How can I rest with my babies lost?"

Jamie started to cry as though hurt at being ignored, and in the bustle of soothing him and giving him some milk and putting him to bed, Seraphina was a little comforted.

They retired to bed saying that there was sure to be good news in the morning, but not one of them slept for an instant. They had left the front door on the latch, and Seraphina kept listening for the sound of steps on the stairs, but there came none.

They rose very early, relieved to be up again, after hours of restless tossing and turning. The usual morning flurry seemed strange without Lexy's help and without Clem's hindrance.

"I'll never call him a nuisance again," moaned Seraphina, "if only he comes back."

"I'll never make Lexy wait on me any more," vowed Cecily, struggling to fasten the hooks down the back of her dress, "if only she'll come back."

They could not touch their breakfast and the landlady did not make matters any better by recounting to them stories of kidnappings and murders, children stolen away by gipsies, and of little bodies found floating in the river.

"Now, make haste, Joshua," pleaded Seraphina, "and see if the police can help you. Why, the children might be at the police station."

"Yes, my love. But I will call in at the theatre on my way, in case there is news."

When he reached the dark little entrance at the back of the theatre the stage-door keeper said, "There's a body to see ye."

Joshua was confronted by an almost spherical figure, muffled up in a strange assortment of wraps and shawls. She had very rosy cheeks and a weatherbeaten face and blue eyes.

"And whan can I do for you, my good lady?" Joshua asked politely.

"I'm wondering if *I* can do *you* a service, sir," she told him. "Is there owt you're missing?"

"Missing?" Joshua scanned her face intently. "Yes, my little son and daughter. D'you know where they are?" He put a hand on her shoulder and peered eagerly into her eyes.

"I do and I do not. There was Bartholomew, the letter-writer, as came to me last night, with a young lass, as he said belonged to a family o' play-actors – neat and tidy, with a fringe of hair on her for'ad."

"That's she – that's my Lexy!" breathed Joshua excitedly.

"And they were enquiring for a little lad – in a peaked cap, with fair curls – "

"That was Clem – And had you seen him?"

She nodded her head.

"Yes, and so I told them. And then some time later back come old Bartholomew. He says they're on the track of the little lad and asks to borrow Ranger, my pony, for an hour or so. 'Yes,' I says, 'and with pleasure.' But he did not bring him back, nor has he this morning, although he knows where I stable Ranger right enough and would have taken him there if he'd returned. And I've heard say this morning that he and your little lady were seen riding along the Chuffham road."

Joshua seemed a little dazed.

"Who is this – Bartholomew?"

"A letter-writer, sir. I've known him these many years. A fine, respectable man. Eddicated, you might say. Oh, he'll take care of the little lass, never you fear."

"So you think they've gone to – Chuffham, searching for Clem?"

"So it sounds, good sir."

Immediately Joshua made up his mind.

"I must ride to Chuffham at once. Now tell me, where are there some livery stables near here that will hire out a horse – no, a horse and trap? I'd best take my wife and daughter with me."

"Where I stable my Ranger they've a trap they do let out now and then."

"Then you shall take me there."

He turned to the door-keeper. "Rehearsal is cancelled for today," he told him. "Make my apologies to the company and assure them that I shall return in time for the show tonight. Come, you shall lead me to the stables." And Joshua set off with the applewoman.

It was soon fixed up for him to hire a smart pony and trap for the day, and he took the applewoman to her stall in the market, and left her there, instructing her to keep her ears and eyes open for news of the children, and in case of anything happening, to send a messenger immediately to the theatre. Then he went to collect Seraphina and Cecily. Seraphina was at a loss to know what to do with Jamie, so they returned to the theatre, in time to catch the other artistes before they had dispersed on hearing of the cancelled rehearsal, and asked the kindly Mrs Tollerton to take charge of Jamie for the day. And then, at last they were able to make for the Chuffham road.

"But why should Clem want to go to Chuffham?" enquired Cecily as they bowled along.

"Oh, perhaps he just made friends with some people, and went off with them. You know he was always doing that when he was younger. I pray to God they be nice people though," said Seraphina earnestly.

It was a beautiful autumn morning, and if their hearts had not been so heavy they would have enjoyed the outing, and the unexpected holiday from rehearsals.

"We must find them," said Joshua, "or we shall have to change tonight's bill. We can't do 'The Dream' without them."

"Is that your only reason for wishing to find them?" demanded Seraphina, rather bitterly.

Joshua made no reply for he knew that her nerves were on edge with fear and anxiety.

It was nearing midday when they reached "The Load of Hay" and Joshua reined in the pony.

"I'll make enquiries here," he said, "and we'll all have a draught of ale."

"Oh, Joshua," cried Seraphina, "this is no time to be supping ale. I don't know how you can think of it – "

Joshua looked at her distraught face and returned with a glass of brandy, which he forced her to drink. Cecily turned up her nose at ale and asked for a glass of port wine and lemonade. When Joshua returned the glasses he made

179

enquiries about Clem and Lexy, and came back to the trap almost running.

"They've been here!" he cried, jumping into the trap and whipping up the pony. "At least they think it was Clem who stayed the night here – and Lexy and this Bartholomew were enquiring for them this morning. On to Chuffham!" cried Joshua in the ringing tones he used in "Henry V" to cry, "Once more unto the breach, dear friends."

"Clem stayed the night there – all by himself?"

"No, my love. With a man from Chuffham, Joe Briggs is his name. We will find them surely now – " He neglected purposely to tell Seraphina the trade that Joe Briggs followed, for he had jumped to the correct conclusion on hearing that Briggs was a sweep.

"But why should anyone steal Clem away like that?" mused Cecily. "He's no good for anything but play-acting. And he's so little – "

"Perhaps it's his hair," moaned Seraphina. "Perhaps they've cut off his lovely curls to sell them – "

Joshua's mouth was set in a firm line as he rehearsed to himself what he should say on meeting Mr Joe Briggs. He even practised cracking the whip a few times.

"Look, Papa!" said Cecily. "There are some gipsies sitting by the road. Tinkers, perhaps. Shall we ask them for news?"

Joshua pulled back the pony to a trot and then a walk. On the grass at the side of the road lay a very old and bony pony, sitting near it an old man with a face lined with the wind and weather, a tousle-headed girl, and a child with a face as black as soot.

When they were still some way away Joshua shouted, "Hey, there, have you by any chance – "

But then he stopped open-mouthed, for the little black-faced creature leaped on to the step and flung himself into Seraphina's lap, and the tousle-headed girl followed suit.

There were such shrieks of delight and laughter and sobs, and even Cecily did not think to tell Clem not to soil her gown.

"I've swept *hundreds* of chimneys this morning," Clem boasted proudly.

"But where is the scoundrel who stole you away?" demanded Joshua.

"Him? Oh, with a lot of sheep," said Clem vaguely.

"Down the road, Papa," Lexy explained. "He was chasing us, but the flock of sheep got in the way, so he gave it up."

"I shall go after him," announced Joshua sternly.

Seraphina laid a hand on his arm.

"No, Joshua!" she implored. "Seeing we are all safe together now, do not let us seek further trouble."

Bartholomew was standing shyly by the apple-woman's pony on the grass verge, and Lexy suddenly remembered him.

"Oh, Papa!" she cried. "You must meet the gentleman who helped me to find Clem. This is Bartholomew, the letter-writer."

Bartholomew bowed very low, and Joshua returned the salute.

"I thank you, sir, with all my heart," said Joshua.

"I have been honoured," was the reply, "to be of service to such a delightful young lady, belonging to such a distinguished family."

"Oh, thank you, thank you," cried Seraphina. "I

dare not think what might have befallen our little ones without your kindly help."

Joshua was a little embarrassed wondering whether or not he should offer the old man any money.

"If I can make recompense in any way – " he began. "If there is anything in the world that I can do for you – " He put his hand into his pocket, but Bartholomew made a gesture of refusal.

"My needs are simple," he said. "I would not accept a gift of money from you, sir. I know how hard the trouping life can be. I was a member of your profession long, long ago, sir. And happy days they were – " He shook his head sadly. "It is always my idle fancy that one day I shall return to the boards, just once before I die."

Joshua slapped his thigh.

"Then, by Jove, that is exactly what you *shall* do. Why do you not come back with us and play with our company for the rest of our stay here? I will pay you whatever you usually make by your letter-writing. That is, of course, if the idea is agreeable to you."

"Agreeable!" Bartholomew could say no more: he was so overcome with joy.

"Oh, hooray. What a fine idea, Papa," cried Lexy. "Won't that be fun, Bartholomew? What part shall he play in tonight's piece, Papa?"

"Let me see – 'The Dream' – Yes, you shall play Philostrate, the master of the games. Old Tollerton usually doubles the part with that of the father, but he will not mind; in fact, he will be glad.'

"A part – " breathed Bartholomew. "After all these years – "

"Come now," said Joshua, "it's time we were

returning. Will you ride in the trap with us, Clem and Lexy? And perhaps our friend will follow behind with the pony."

"It wasn't a very nice pony," observed Clem. "Its bones stuck out in very uncomfortable places. You're much more comfortable," he told his mother in whose lap he was sitting. She hugged him regardless of the soot.

When they reached "The Load of Hay" they stopped and went inside for a meal, for all were suddenly feeling extremely hungry. They had a large leg of mutton with caper sauce and roast potatoes and a blackberry and apple pie with farmhouse cream. Clem sank back in his chair exhausted.

"That's one bad thing about being a chimney-sweep," he observed. "You don't seem to eat much."

When they returned to the theatre, the company was just beginning to drift in for the evening show. They embraced Clem and Lexy as though they had been missing for years, and cast curious glances at Bartholomew. They seemed doubtful at first when Joshua told them that Bartholomew was to play with the company for the remainder of their stay at Shefferton. But Bartholomew was so obviously enchanted at the prospect and so admiring and respectful to all of them that they soon warmed to him. He was given a little slip of a dressing-room to himself, and Joshua lent him some make-up. Fortunately he was much the same size as Matthew Tollerton, so his robes fitted him.

"Oh, it is lovely to be back!" Lexy sighed as she bustled round, doing half a dozen things at once.

Clem was at last persuaded to wash so that his make-up would go on properly, and eventually they were all ready for the curtain to rise.

Bartholomew was so nervous that he was trembling

like a leaf and telling everyone it was fifty years since he'd trod the boards. Then the tinny orchestra, consisting of a fiddle, a 'cello and an out-of-tune piano, struck up the overture, and the court of Theseus got into their places for the opening scene. The overture ended and the curtain rose to show this dignified tableau.

Suddenly from the wings appeared a strange, dumpy figure, gazing around her in bewilderment, quite unaware that she had strayed on to the stage. Suddenly she saw Bartholomew.

"Why, Bartholomew," cried the applewoman loudly, "what *are* you doing got up like that? I've come for me pony."

CHAPTER 10

The "Robber's" Return

A letter lay on Cecily's plate at breakfast time. It was in a pale pink envelope with fluted edges, and written in a flowing hand in mauve ink.

The rest of the family sat and looked anxiously at it, waiting for Cecily, who was last as usual, to come down. It was quite an event for any of them to receive a letter, for they moved about so quickly that even if anyone wrote it hardly ever caught up with them.

"Mamma, will Cecily let me have the pretty envelope to make a paper boat?" Clem demanded.

"I don't doubt it, my love. But do not finger it now."

Even Jamie stretched out a plump fist and tried to claim it as a plaything. At last Cecily appeared, sleepy-eyed, yawning and complaining. "Mercy, how I hate the mornings. They are so early – " Then she saw her letter and swooped on it with a cry of joy. As she read it the colour surged up into her cheeks and her eyes filled, although she was smiling with joy and excitement.

"Mamma, Papa," she cried, "it is fwom the Honouwable Poppy Pagett. She asks me to pass a few weeks with them. They are to have a house party – oh, please say that I may – "

Joshua drained the tankard of porter that he always drank at breakfast.

"And how, might I ask, do you intend to get there? Where does this lady reside? Buxton, is it not? It would cost you a pretty penny to reach there, my child. And, also, we cannot spare you from the bill. A few weeks, indeed – You must curb your cravings for an idle life. It does not befit a play-actor's child!"

"But, Papa – "

"Those are my last words – " and Joshua got up and left the table, obviously distressed at having to be so harsh.

Cecily's face slowly fell, and then she burst into tears, with her head on the breakfast table. Jamie joined in from sympathy, and Clem banged his spoon on the table shouting, "Cry baby cry – Stick your finger in your eye – "

"Mamma, why is Papa so cwuel?" wailed Cecily. "I never get any enjoyment and gaiety as other young girls do. And how here's my opportunity – and Papa says no – "

Once more she was immersed in floods of tears. Lexy patted her shoulder helplessly and Seraphina looked very sad.

"Dear child," she said gently, "I know that what you say is true and I am very, very sorry. But there is no help for it. We are a poor family. And it is something for a poor girl not to be forced to do manual work like the young girls in the mills and the mines. I know you miss your old school friends, and if only there were some way of allowing you to go I should be so happy for you."

Cecily would not be comforted. She wept and wailed

until Clem said in an interested tone, "Look, Cecily, you're making splashes on the tablecloth."

Then she ran from the room, sobbing loudly.

"Clem," said Lexy, "you should not have said that."

"Well, she *was* making splashes. Jolly big ones."

Lexy followed Cecily up to the bedroom and found her crying on the bed.

"You'd best hurry," she said, "or we'll be late for rehearsal and Papa will be angry."

"I hate Papa – " stormed Cecily. "He does not love me – He does not mind if I die an old maid – "

"But what has that to do with the Honourable Poppy Pagett's party?"

"What has it got to do with it?" Cecily nearly screeched at her. "Mr Horton will be there – " She finished on a despairing wail.

"Oh," said Lexy; "oh, I see." She walked over to the window and stared out at the grim view of roofs and chimney stacks.

"And he'll surely find another girl and – oh dear – " Cecily's voice once more became muffled with sobs. At last they became quieter and she sat up on the bed and said very seriously, "I hate this life. I love Mamma and Papa and you and the little boys, but I hate this life. I'm just not meant for it. All this work and to-do just about one silly old play after another. And as for that Shakespeare – I hate him more than evewything else put together. And all this talk about 'the show must go on'. I don't care if it *never* goes on, ever any more. You and I and Mamma and Papa have all sacwificed too much alweady over it."

Lexy was horrified.

"But – but what else *is* there?" she asked.

"Life – " cried Cecily. "People and fun and balls and clothes and parties and – and getting mawwied and living in a house – not these eternal lodgings and landladies – and nothing but studying lines."

Lexy sighed and shook her head.

"It's no good, Cecily," she said, "I just can't imagine anything else."

"I know, poor lamb." Cecily's face softened a little. "But Mamma said she had a wonderful time when she was in London before she mawwied Papa, although she was on the stage."

"But she doesn't seem to mind being married to Papa – "

"She still thinks he's a gweat actor – " Cecily scanned Lexy's face. "Do you, Lexy? If he is, then why are we so poor? Why do so few people come to see him?"

Lexy had never really thought about this before. She had always taken it for granted that her father was a great actor. It was just that they were always beset by bad luck. She thought about this as she mechanically tidied up the bedroom and then she said, "I don't really care much whether Papa is a great actor or not. He is Papa, and I love him dearly, and I cannot judge him as an actor."

"But do you not see – " urged Cecily, "if there is nothing gweat about him, then why is he wasting all our lives dwagging us about from town to town?"

"What would you have him do? Settle down and have a – a grocer's shop?"

"A twadesman? Mercy no – he could be – he could – well – "

"What could he be?" demanded Lexy. "Papa could be nothing but an actor – "

188

"Well, I shall never be an actwess – I know it," said Cecily, turning over sulkily on to her face.

Lexy could not get this conversation out of her head. It was the first time that Cecily had ever talked to her as though they were equals. She had thought that Cecily was beginning to settle down and to accept their way of living, but the invitation from the Honourable Poppy Pagget had made it quite clear that this was not so. Ten times a day the letter in the pink envelope was brought out and re-read with many sighs and tears.

"But how did she ever find your address?" Lexy wanted to know.

"It just so happened that I had written to her the week before and told her where we would be – " Cecily sighed heavily, "but perhaps it is a blessing I am not to visit her, for what should I wear? And look at my hands – " She spread them out despairingly. "Doing all the washing and sewing will be the wuination of them."

Lexy nearly gasped with surprise to hear Cecily say that she did all the washing and sewing, for if she washed so much as a napkin for Jamie or sewed on a bonnet string it was an occurrence to remark upon.

Joshua and Seraphina did their best to cheer their elder daughter by letting her play all her favourite parts, which were of course the smallest, and by admiring every new style of coiffure that she adopted, but she continued to mope and sigh and look pale until even the company began to comment upon it. Courtney Stanton was honestly of the opinion that Miss Mannering was about to fall into a decline, and brought her bottles of iron tonic to improve her blood.

"Impwove my blood, indeed!" snapped Cecily, turning up her nose at the gift. Nowadays the attentions of

189

the juvenile lead that used to flatter her seemed to enrage her and soon she was treating him so badly that he too began to grow melancholy.

"The girl will ruin the company," lamented Joshua. "Before she came back we were a sane, hard-working troupe. Now she is turning it into – a background to a novelette. I will not have this wilting about and these poetic languors."

For Lexy it just meant more work. If Cecily retired to bed with the vapours then everything had to be done by Lexy. She began to play several of the parts that Cecily had been used to playing, even the part of the girl in "The Clown's Revenge", which was the most grown-up part that Lexy had ever played.

"And a sight better than that lily-livered sister of yours," Matthew Tollerton told her after the first performance she gave, and kissed her on both cheeks. "You've a turn for comedy, child, with that funny little face of yours."

One day in November Joshua came on to the stage before the morning rehearsal, waving a letter.

"Good news, my friends," he said. "A request from the manager of the Marlingford Theatre, asking that I will bring my troupe there for Christmas and put on a Christmas play to open on Boxing Night. They do not want any vulgar burlesque or pantomime – but a tasteful and spectacular piece, and he is willing to help with the expense of putting it on. He particularly asks that there should be good parts in it for the children, so that young people will be brought to see it during their holidays from their studies. Fortune smiles, my friends."

There was an immediate buzz of relief from the

company for they had been wondering for a long time where Christmas would find them.

"Marlingford," said Seraphina. "I shall never forget our last visit. Was it not there that we suffered the dreadful fire?"

"I wish we might stay at the Red Lion again," sighed Cecily. "It was the only time I have been warm since I rejoined the troupe."

"Were you not warm at Scanchester?" demanded Joshua. "As I remember, it was warm enough."

"I mean comfortable," said Cecily.

"Well, we shall see – " said Joshua jovially. "The terms offered are generous, I may say. Perhaps you may see the Red Lion once more."

"Oh Joshua, how delightful," cried Seraphina. "What a happy Christmas that would be – "

"I must find someone to write us a Christmas show – some tasteful extravaganza – the people at Marlingford are refined in their tastes, you remember, and we were well supported by the gentry – Something with fairies I think – " Joshua paced the stage, deep in thought.

"It must have a good part for me, Papa!" stipulated Clem.

"It shall, my little man. And perhaps, yes, perhaps a part for Jamie – as a changeling child, perhaps stolen by the fairies."

"Oh, no, Papa – " Cecily was horrified. "Such a mite cannot be cawwied on to a dusty dwaughty stage – !"

"Nonsense!" said Seraphina. "The sooner he starts, the better. I made my first appearance when I was five days old. My mother had left the show and gone to stay at *her* mother's for a while and there I was born. When I was five

191

days old she brought me to the theatre while the show was in progress and put me in the arms of one of the walking ladies in the wings while she went to find my father. But she missed him, and he encountered the walking lady with me in her arms just as he was about to make his entrance. His was a comic act you will remember, and he laughingly picked me from the good lady's arms, and carried me on to the stage in order to make some quip to the audience. As he came off again my mother came running into the wings, and when she saw him she said. 'You've not taken that baby on the boards?' 'Yes, m'dear! Why not? It's a nice wee thing!' he said laughing. 'But, it's yours – it's ours – it's Seraphina – ' she said, and they say that his face was a picture to see.''

Lexy had heard this story many times over but she always loved to hear about her mother's parents because it gave her a feeling of having relations – grandparents, aunts and cousins – just like other children, although both her parents' relatives were long since dead.

The whole company was looking forward to the return to Marlingford and to the opportunity to settle down for a few weeks together, instead of the incessant journeying of the last few months. Cecily was a little comforted for missing her visit to the Pagetts', but kept saying, "If I had gone there when I was invited, why, they might even have asked me to stay for Christmas!"

"But it will be pleasant at Marlingford at the Red Lion – remember how we enjoyed it before – and a new play for Christmas – "

"So long as I don't have to be a faiwy," said Cecily petulantly. "It's all vewy well for you and Clem to fly about on wires, but it makes me feel ill and the harness bwuises me shockingly. I will tell Papa I wefuse to do it."

Joshua soon informed the company that they were to travel to Marlingford the week before Christmas and would have several days of rehearsal for the fantasy, with no shows in the evenings. This was luxury for them, and Joshua impressed upon them that he would expect a higher standard of performance than ever.

They were all very merry on the journey to Marlingford, going through the lines of the play that Joshua had commissioned a London author to write for them. It was called "The Enchanted Glade, or A Christmas Night's Wonder", and, as the theatre manager had stipulated, the children's parts were the best. Clem played a little boy who had been stolen away by the gnomes as a baby (Jamie representing the baby in the early scenes). Lexy was to be a bad gnome, and Cecily a good fairy (with her hair down, but not a flying fairy). Joshua and Seraphina were the sorrowing mother and father; Mrs Tollerton, a witch (rather a better nourished one than most, Lexy reflected), and her husband a surly wizard. Barney Fidgett was to play several villagers and Courtney Stanton the village youth who falls fruitlessly in love with the good fairy without realising that she is not a mortal.

The play was voted "sweetly pretty" by all the company, except Clem, who only said in a disappointed tone, "No blood – "

Joshua had already written to the Red Lion to reserve rooms for the family and the landlord was waiting in the yard to greet them when their cab drove in. It gave Lexy a warm feeling inside to see that they were wanted some-

193

where, and Joshua waved his hat in a grand gesture as he got out of the cab.

"Perhaps he *is* a great actor – " thought Lexy, as she watched the landlord treating her father with the deference due to a celebrity.

"And your nestlings – " cried the landlord jovially, "how have ye been faring since last we saw your little faces? Has it been a triumphal tour, sir, I'm hoping?"

"Triumphal, yes, triumphal – " laughed Joshua, radiant and proud as he helped them to descend. The horrors of fever at Scanchester, poverty at Huncaster, and kidnapping at Shefferton were quite forgotten.

They were to stay in the same rooms they had occupied on their last visit and it was wonderful to be there without the terror of the fire fresh in their memories. Lexy felt that she loved every beam of the old place.

It was while they sat down to a meal in the long low-raftered dining-room that a very important occurrence took place. Jamie, who was propped up on his mother's knee looked long and solemnly at his father and then said very clearly, "Papa – "

The whole family shrieked with joy and surprise, and, once having discovered the delights of conversation, Jamie would not stop. He went on to say, "Mum – Mum – ", and even "Sis" to Cecily, and all the other guests crowded round to hear this sudden flow of speech. Then, exhausted, he quite suddenly fell asleep and Lexy took him upstairs and tucked him into his basket.

Although the prospects of a few days without shows had seemed like luxury, there was so much to be done on the Christmas play that they were rehearsing until midnight on several occasions. Seraphina would not allow Jamie to be used for late rehearsals. He was a distraction anyhow, as now that he had suddenly discovered how to talk there was no stopping him, and he would gabble "Mum, Mum, Pa – Pa – " and "Sis – Sis – " all through everyone's speeches. The dummy which, wrapped in one of Jamie's shawls, they used when he was not present was much more accommodating. One day Lexy went to Jamie's basket in the dressing-room, and was horrified to find tucked into it, not her little brother, but the dummy – With a cry of horror she ran to one of the property chests and opened the lid. Sure enough, on top of a pile of property dishes and imitation fruit lay Jamie, fast asleep.

"Who put Jamie down just this minute?" she went round the family demanding.

"Eh, what's that?" said her father absent-mindedly. "It was I. The little fellow seemed tired."

"But you put him in the property chest and the dummy is in the basket," expostulated Lexy.

"Nonsense, nonsense, you're getting confused, child. Now I want to go back on the finale of the last act."

Lexy sighed and reflected that at least her father had the absence of mind of a genius. She did not tell her mother, as she knew she would be upset, and they had experienced enough of Cecily saying when they were last in Marlingford that a theatre was no place for a baby. And Jamie seemed to have slept just as well in the property chest –

The remainder of the week passed in a whirl of rehearsal and preparations for Christmas. Lexy had received her weekly pocket-money of twopence a few days early, in order to be able to buy her Christmas gifts for the family. Whenever she had a moment she slipped out into the streets to press her nose against the bow windows of the shops

195

which seemed to be bulging out towards the pavements more than usual, so full were they of good things for Christmas. The butchers' windows were fairly bursting with turkeys and geese and whole pigs, and the grocers' with candied peel and dried fruits or Christmas cakes and puddings. It was very difficult to decide what to get. Eventually Lexy decided on a pincushion in the shape of a heart for her mother, a cheroot for her father, who, although refusing throughout the year to have any truck with the habit of smoking, always allowed himself one cigar on Christmas Day. The only one that Lexy could afford was not at all good, and she hoped that it would not injure his throat.

While she was scanning the drapers' windows for something for Cecily, she heard the sound of music in the busy street, and there in the gutter was a dancing bear on a long chain, led by his master. The man played a flute, and the bear made rather sad dancing movements lumbering along on his hind legs, splashed by mud thrown up by the horses' hooves and the wheels of passing vehicles. Lexy felt very sorry for him and gave him one of the sugarplums she had bought for Clem. For Cecily she bought some new bonnet strings, and then having spent a half-penny on each of the family but the baby, she had exhausted her wealth. For Jamie she would have to make a woolly toy before Christmas Day. She sighed and wished that her gifts might have been a little more sumptuous. Then she hurried back into the theatre to practise her "flying".

The dress rehearsal of "The Enchanted Glade" was fixed for Christmas Day itself, but would not begin until after the Christmas dinner had been eaten at midday at the Red Lion. Joshua had arranged for the rest of the company, who were not staying at the Lion, to come in to join them.

On Christmas Eve it was getting on for midnight when they returned to the inn, but there were fires glowing in their rooms, and the whole shadowy house seemed to Lexy to be waiting for Christmas to dawn. Clem was wild with excitement and insisted on hanging up his bolster-case, although his parents assured him that Santa Claus would never be able to carry enough down the chimney to fill it.

"I shall not hang up my stocking," Cecily announced. "I am too old for such nonsense."

"Oh, yes, do," pleaded Lexy, "it will be so much better in the morning if you have a stocking too – I shall feel silly if it's only me."

"Vewy well, then," she assented quite readily, "just to please you."

For the first time since Cecily had rejoined the family, Lexy thought, as they lay in bed watching the shadows that the fire-light threw on to the ceiling, how nice it was to have a sister to share things with. Lexy had never been taught to believe in fairies or in Santa Claus either for Joshua thought that it was bad for a child to be told untruths even about such matters, but there was still something almost magical about the way that an empty stocking suddenly became full and lumpy and exciting by Christmas morning. And before she seemed to have had time to finish this thought it actually *was* Christmas morning, and Clem was bouncing on top of her, dragging with him his bolster-case, heavy with packages.

"I've come in here to open mine with you – " he shouted, "but I shan't give you any of my presents."

"I've got some of my own, thank you," said Lexy, scrambling down to the end of the bed to find her stocking and Cecily's.

197

Cecily had to be shaken before she would wake up enough to take any interest. Then in came Joshua and Seraphina, still in their gowns, with Jamie crowing in his mother's arms, to give a Christmas kiss to everyone, and to watch the unwrapping of the gifts. Although the presents were small and not costly they were all delighted with them. Most of the company had given something to each of them, and the landlord had provided the basis of the stockings – a good layer of oranges and nuts and sweeties. Clem was thrilled with a painted wooden horse that took up most of his bolster-case. It had real fur stuck on for a mane, and stripes of blue and red on its back and a handle behind so that its rider could be wheeled around on it. Clem soon had his father pushing him riotously round and round the room. Cecily had a shawl in a pretty shade of mauve from her parents, and she expressed delight at the bonnet strings from Lexy, which just matched it. Lexy could not make out what the large knobbly parcel that filled the top of her stocking could be. When she unwrapped it she found that it was a beautifully fitted sewing-basket with a little pair of scissors, a tape-measure that came out of a holder shaped like a strawberry, and needles and bodkins of every shape and size. It was the loveliest gift she had ever had. From Clem she had a bag of very sticky humbugs.

"I sucked one or two just to see they were all right," he explained. "That's why they're sticky!"

Lexy thanked him gravely and offered him some, and was relieved to find that by breakfast-time he had finished off the whole bag.

It was very late before they were up, washed and dressed.

"I'm not having much for breakfast," declared Clem, "so that I can stuff at dinner-time."

"And very wise," his father told him. "We shall follow your shining example and all partake of a frugal breakfast."

No sooner did breakfast seem to be over than the

rest of the company arrived ready for the Christmas dinner. They had all brought a little something to add to it – a bottle of port, a bag of nuts, a box of sugared peel. While the landlord and his wife finished preparing the goose, they all sat round the big open fire, roasting chestnuts. And then the door was flung open, and in came the landlord, carrying an enormous goose on a platter. Behind him came his wife bearing a turkey and behind her all the servants that the inn could muster carrying side plates of delicacies to surround the poultry. There was bread sauce and stuffing, and boatsful of gravy – potatoes roast, potatoes in their jackets and potatoes boiled. Clem surveyed the crowded table and said sadly, "I don't think my inside will be big enough!"

And when they had eaten their fill of the birds, on came a collection of jellies, tartlets and mince pies, and as centrepiece an enormous Christmas pudding. It was quite a monster with a large sprig of holly sticking in the top, and brandy poured over it and lit so that it flamed in beautiful colours of orange and blue.

Lexy ate silently and thankfully, remembering "bones for the dog" at Scanchester and trying to stoke up for any similarly hungry day that would probably occur in the future.

"Thank you, God," she remembered to say, when they said grace at the end of meal, "for letting me be full today at all events."

The landlord was all for keeping them round the tables cracking nuts and telling stories, but Joshua shook his head, and reminded his replete company that there was a dress rehearsal to be gone through.

"And," he added, "I have been asked to tell you by

our friend the theatre manager that we have all been invited
to a Christmas party tonight at – oh, the name eludes me –
at any rate, it is a mansion some way out of the town owned
by some local people of quality who have kindly asked that
any of us who care to should attend. They are sending a
carriage for us at eight o'clock. So – should the rehearsal
be over – any who feel so inclined may go. I myself intend
to retire early."

"Oh, Papa – " gasped Cecily, "why did you not tell
us before? How could you keep such a thing to yourself? I
may go, may I not? Oh, please Papa – a Chwistmas party
at a mansion – "

"That depends, dear girl, on who there may be to
escort you – "

It seemed that nobody else but Courtney Stanton
was anxious to go.

"My dancing days are over," avowed Mrs Tollerton.
"Thirty years ago I'd have jumped at the chance – even after
a dress rehearsal. Let the young people go, my dear – " she
urged Seraphina.

"But it would not look well for just two of them to
arrive unchaperoned at the house of people of quality," said
Seraphina. "But *I* have nothing to wear – "

"Then let Lexy go too!" said Mrs Tollerton comfort-
ably. "It will make an outing for the child."

"Lexy!" gasped Cecily, "But she is not 'out' yet; she
is only a child."

"They will expect a little strangeness from play-
actors," said Gertrude Tollerton, "probably that is why they
have invited us. But Lexy is a better chaperone than none
– and Christmas night is the time for children to go to
parties. Have a heart, Seraphina."

201

Seraphina looked at Joshua, who was so mellow after his enormous meal that he nodded. Cecily waltzed round the room with delight. Courtney Stanton quoted nearly the whole of the balcony scene, and Lexy suddenly felt very sick.

"But – but I've nothing to wear – " she gasped.

"Your blue velveteen will be very suitable," said Seraphina. "Children should not be too frilled up for a grown-up party."

"But what shall *I* wear?" demanded Cecily. "All my gowns are so shabby now – "

"I have it!" said Mrs Tollerton. "Why do you not wear your fairy dress from the play? It is sweetly pretty and without the wings it really is quite in the mode."

"It is a trifle transparent," objected Joshua. "Such things are suitable on the boards but not in a ballroom."

"Fiddlesticks!" said Gertrude Tollerton. "You should see some of the gowns these fashionable ladies wear – a ballet girl would blush with shame. You wear your fairy dress, my girl, and enchant the lot of them."

Cecily was pink in the face with excitement.

"Yes, I will. Oh, how glorious to dance again. Do you waltz, Mr Stanton?"

"Ardently – Miss Mannering," was the reply with such a gallant gesture that Clem giggled. He was only interested in the food involved.

"Will there be ice cream, do you think?" he asked longingly. The children had never tasted ice cream, and it was one of his ambitions to sample this rare delicacy.

"I expect so," said Seraphina, "it is always a feature of a fashionable ball." She sighed rather sadly.

"We must away," said Joshua, "if we are to get our day's work done."

The landlord promised to leave a bowl of hot punch and some sandwiches for their return, as it was sure to be late, either from rehearsal or from the party.

Lexy carried her blue velveteen over to the theatre, casting nervous glances at the worn patches. She was half excited and half terrified at the prospect of going to a real grown-up party – she who had never even been to a children's party.

During every lull in the dress rehearsal Cecily was ironing the drapery of her fairy dress, and crimping her hair with tongs. She tried to do Lexy's hair too, but Joshua objected.

"Gnomes may not have ringlets – or frizz," he said. "Leave her hair be – "

Cecily missed so many entrances because she was posing in front of the mirror without her wings on to see if her dress looked fashionable, that normally Joshua would have been furious; but Seraphina kept reminding him that this little outing would make up for the loss of her visit to the Pagetts'.

Lexy's head was in a whirl. What with trying to remember her lines as the gnome, and her flying entrances and exits, and helping with the properties and effects, and wondering whether clean gloves with darns were better than grubby ones without, she could not remember ever having such a bewildering day.

The dress rehearsal followed the pattern of most dress rehearsals. Joshua said beforehand, "Now we will go straight through the piece without a single halt," but by six o'clock in the evening they still had not finished the first

203

act. Scenery would not stand up properly, costumes were found unsuitable and had to be altered, and then something went wrong with the gas foot-lighting, and they had to finish their rehearsal by candle light.

At last, at eight, Joshua said, "That will be all for the main part of the company. Be in the theatre early tomorrow for there will be endless details to be attended to. Now we will rehearse the Harlequinade, and those not concerned may go."

"Dear Papa," cried Cecily and flew from the stage to get ready.

When Lexy had changed from her gnome's tunic into her blue velveteen she looked despairingly at herself in the glass; that hair – those teeth – and the poor shabby dress – She heaved a sigh, and tried to remember that this party was not for her benefit, but for Cecily's and her own rôle was merely that of chaperone.

Cecily was looking radiant in her pink and gold fairy's dress, wearing a pair of long gloves lent by Seraphina, a very beautiful old fan of Mrs Tollerton's and with her new shawl draped elegantly over her white shoulders.

"The material of that dress looks better from a distance," said Seraphina, "so do not go too near to other folk in conversation. Keep your distance and they will not realise that it is but tarlatan and tinsel."

"What of me, Mamma? I should keep the distance of the room between me and other folk," said Lexy "Look at the worn patches on my dress."

"It only wants steaming up over a kettle – here, child – "

Seraphina lit a spirit-stove in the dressing-room and

placing a kettle on it, instructed Lexy to revolve slowly in
the steam that would come from the spout.

"Ow," squealed Lexy, "it's burning me through the
dress."

"Of course it will," scolded Joshua. "You pack of
half-witted women! Now that's enough of your prinking.
Off to the party with you or I'll go through the third act
once more."

"Spare us!" cried Cecily. "Lexy, go and fetch
Courtney Stanton. Tell him we are weady."

Courtney Stanton was craning his neck in his dressing
room in an effort to see both sides of his profile at once.
He was looking very fine in a beautifully-cut evening suit
that Lexy had never been him wear before. He looked
rather doubtfully at her blue velveteen.

"I've got some gloves," Lexy said apologetically,
"but I'm not putting them on until I get there, because of
getting them soiled. Cecily is ready."

When Courtney saw Cecily he bowed very low, and
produced from behind his back a beautiful bouquet of Christmas roses all done up in fancy paper. Cecily accepted
them with the air of a princess receiving homage from a
subject, and then dispatched him to find her wrap. Their
shabby cloaks rather spoiled the picture, but Cecily threw
her shawl loosely over her head and shoulders and floated
out of the dressing-room leaving Seraphina and Mrs
Tollerton shaking their heads sentimentally.

"Do bring me back an ice-cream," said Clem
wistfully.

Outside the theatre stood a very handsome carriage,
with a footman on a little step at the back. He leaped down

and opened the door for them, saying, "You'll be the party for the Hall?"

"That is so!" said Cecily in her most queenly manner.

The carriage was beautifully upholstered inside, and as they bowled along the deserted streets Lexy pretended that she was Queen Victoria and bowed to left and right, until Cecily and Courtney noticed and laughed at her.

At length they turned up a drive through some heavy, ornate gates with a lodge beside them. At the end of the drive stood a very large mansion, with lights in every window, and as the carriage came to a standstill the sound of music floated out through the windows.

"We don't even know who to ask for!" murmured Cecily.

"Perhaps we should just enter and say, 'the actors are come hither'," quoted Courtney.

"They would expect us to walk in on our hands and do a few back-spwings."

"In all probability that is what they expect anyhow – "

Lexy had never felt so terrified in her life as when they approached the massive front door. It was already held open by a flunkey in a very splendid livery. The hall was enormous and paved with mosaic, and there were chandeliers, and a broad marble staircase. It was like the set to "Little Sir Randolph" only more solid, Lexy thought. And suddenly Lexy was very, very glad that she had spent all her life on the stage, because she felt that she knew how to behave in these strange surroundings merely by remembering pieces out of various plays they had done. She had known that the flunkey was a flunkey because she had seen old Barney Fidgett in that rôle so many times, wearing a costume just like that. And now as a very beautiful lady descended the staircase, with two gentlemen behind her, she guessed that this must be their hostess, and she hastily thought through all the plays of society life that she knew to find the right words with which to greet her. The lady sailed forward to meet them. She was blazing with jewels and smiling very graciously.

"You are the theatre troupe?" she enquired. "Miss Mannering, is it not?"

"Yes, ma'am. And this is my little sister, Alexandwa."

"Delighted to have the pleasure of your acquaintance," said Lexy seriously.

"How charming!" cried their hostess, and turned to Courtney Stanton.

"Courtney Stanton, ma'am – at your service," said he, and bowed very low (straight from "A Tale of Two Cities" thought Lexy).

"Allow me to present my husband, Sir Bartlett Horton."

An elderly gentleman with white side-whiskers stepped forward and bowed.

"And my son – "

Lexy gasped – for the handsome, smiling young man who stepped forward and lifted Cecily's hand to his lips was none other than Mr Horton – Cecily's Mr Horton, "The robber" –

"You have already met, of course?" said Lady Horton. "At the Pagetts', was it not?"

"Yes, it was," said Cecily, suddenly going so pale that Lexy thought she was about to faint.

"When I heard that your father's troupe would be at

Marlingford for Christmas I instructed Mamma that she must extend an invitation to you all for tonight,'' said Mr Horton casually enough, but his eyes never left Cecily's.

"Your ladyship is as gracious as she is beautiful,'' said Lexy, from the second act of "Little Sir Randolph'', to fill in the pause that had suddenly occurred.

"What a quaint mite!'' exclaimed Lady Horton. "Now come and I will show you where to leave your wraps.''

Lexy could see that her quick eyes had taken in the shabbiness of their cloaks and their heavy boots. She was glad to be able to get out of them into her dancing pumps in the spacious bedroom at the top of the marble staircase, where there was pile upon pile of sumptuous fur cloaks and satin-lined wraps. A maid was in attendance, helping the ladies to smooth their hair and offering pins to repair any mishap to dance dresses.

"How delightful!'' cried Lady Horton as Cecily took off her wrap. "What an original dress! I have not seen one quite like it before.''

She advanced to study the material more closely, but Cecily darted across to Lexy and started to arrange her hair.

As they descended to the ballroom Lady Horton gave them each a little card – a programme of the order of the dances – with a little pencil attached by a gilt string. Lexy thought they were very sweet, but could not guess their purpose.

"What are they for?'' she whispered to Cecily.

"When anyone wants to dance with you, he puts his name down on the card against the dance for which he is claiming you.''

Mr Horton and Courtney Stanton joined them at the foot of the staircase, and Mr Horton offered Cecily his arm and Courtney offered his to their hostess. Lexy trailed behind as they made for the ballroom where an orchestra was playing a waltz.

Lexy could scarcely believe her eyes. So this was the effect that her father had been striving to obtain in the ballroom scenes of "The False Marquess". The couples swirling by, the little gilt chairs standing in conversational groups along the walls, the palms, the delicious perfumes that wafted from the beautifully-dressed ladies – it was all such a perfect stage effect that it made Lexy want to cry.

Mr Horton was writing busily in Cecily's dance programme, while Courtney Stanton, after polite conversation with his hostess, also tried to get his name down for as many dances as possible on Cecily's programme.

Then Mr Horton turned to Lexy, "Now, what is your favourite dance, Miss Lexy? A waltz, a polka, a cotillion?"

"Polka," said Lexy shyly, for she could just remember that a polka went 1-2-3-hop.

Mr Horton wrote his name down on her card for the next polka, and then said to Cecily, "This is our dance, I believe, Miss Mannering," and off they sailed together.

"If I might have the pleasure – " said Courtney Stanton to Lady Horton, and off they twirled as well. Lexy went and perched on one of the litttle gilt chairs which looked so much like stage furniture that she was surprised to find it so solid, and she looked and looked at everyone and everything so hard that her eyes felt as if they would come unfixed. And all the time she could not believe that it was really happening – she kept feeling that it was all a beautifully staged extravaganza, just for her benefit. When the dance was finished and everyone had clapped and said, "How delightful," Mr Horton and Cecily came back to her.

"It is our polka next," said Mr Horton with his friendly smile. "Do not forget, Lexy!"

"As if I would!" thought Lexy.

When the music began again he bowed very low, and then offered her his arm. Lexy reached up and took it, and he walked her right to the centre of the floor before commencing to dance. Lexy had had to dance the polka once on the stage in one of the burlesques, so she was fairly confident, and Mr Horton was a very good dancer.

"You are as light as a fairy!" he told her as they swung round. She could not help looking at their reflection in the long mirrors that lined the wall, giving an impression of an endless ballroom stretching into eternity. Her dress did not look quite right beside all the other silks and satins, but at least they did the polka as well as any couple on the floor. A lot of people stopped to look at them, and Mr Horton smiled or waved an airy hand and really seemed to be enjoying himself.

"Have you had any refreshment yet?" he enquired.

"No," said Lexy. "Is there some?"

"Why, yes, in the supper-room. Let us all go there after this dance, before it becomes too crowded."

"Oh, well," thought Lexy, as the gay polka had come to an end, "I may have worked hard the year round, but I'm having as good a Christmas night as any girl could wish for."

As they entered the supper-room Lexy exclaimed aloud. It did not look like a buffet so much as a bower. There was a long, long table stretched across one end of the room, and on it was such an array of exciting foodstuffs that Lexy felt really sorry that Clem was not there, for he would have appreciated it so. There were whole cold

210

chickens and ducks in aspic jelly, and jellies and blancmanges of all shapes and sizes. And tarts and mince pies and bowls of fruit all piled up (just like stage properties, thought Lexy again). And right in the middle was an enormous bowl of pure white cream stuff, and on top of it in pink lettering the words "A Merry Christmas".

"Cecily," whispered Lexy, "is that – is it ice cream?"

"Why, yes, of course. But don't ask for it first, or it will look ill-mannered."

Mr Horton and Courtney Stanton brought them plates of cold duck and goose and turkey, and offered them tarts and trifles and fruit, and Lexy went manfully through them all, but all the time anxious to get on to the magical bowl of ice cream. At last she said timidly when Mr Horton asked what she would have, "I'll try a morsel of ice cream, if you please."

When it arrived she smelt it and looked at it and would like to have licked at it with her tongue, but she received a warning glance from Cecily, and used the little silver spoon instead. It was cold – colder than she had ever imagined and quite, quite delicious. Cecily was eating it in a very disinterested fashion and even left some in her cut-glass bowl. Lexy was still under the spell of ice cream when the others were anxious to get back to the dance floor.

"You remain here, Lexy, and finish your ice," said Cecily, "and we will return for you."

Lexy nodded gently, trying to keep the coldness of the ice from stinging her teeth. When she had finished the bowl she felt too full to have more, although the servants were serving it to anyone who wished it. She thought of how Clem would have loved it, and decided that by hook or by crook she would take some home to him. Approaching the buffet she indicated the bowl of ice cream and was glad when they gave her a very hard, firm, well-iced portion that had the letter "C" of Christmas on it in pink. Clem would think that it stood for his name. She took it over into the far corner of the room, and, when nobody was looking in her direction, she transferred it from its bowl into a table-napkin that was lying on a side table. This she folded up neatly and put into her pocket, which was detachable and hung from the waist of her dress like a purse-bag. Then she made her way out of the supper-room and went and sat at the edge of the dance floor. By this time she was getting rather sleepy. After a dress rehearsal and two meals of considerably larger proportions than she usually ate in a whole week, her strength had been somewhat over-taxed, and soon the music and the bright swirling couples began to merge into a long, seemingly endless belt that revolved and revolved.

She was wakened by an unpleasant sensation of water dripping over her. Looking down at her lap she exclaimed softly to herself. In her lap, seeping through the fold of table-napkin and through her blue velveteen pocket came a thin stream of watery ice cream. It lay in a pool in her lap, mixed with the pink of the lettering and the blue colouring that was coming out of her dress. She looked guiltily round the dance floor. Cecily was dancing rather closer to Mr Horton than she had been when Lexy had last noticed them, and Courtney Stanton stood scowling in a corner watching them. Lexy looked wildly round for some way of escape. If she stood up there would be a pool of ice cream on that beautifully polished floor. She could have kicked herself for not realising that ice cream would melt. And then she saw that in one corner of the ballroom a small glass door led into some sort of conservatory, where there were potted palms and ferns. If only she could get there, she could pour the ice cream into a flowerpot and mop herself down with the dry parts of the table-napkin. Suddenly inspired she picked up the corners of her skirt, so that the pool in the middle would not spill, and waltzed demurely in time to the music all by herself to the conservatory doorway. Anyone who noticed her merely thought: "What a quaint child to dance all by herself."

Mercifully the conservatory was empty. She drained the ice cream into a flowerpot, hoping that it would not kill the aspidistra that it contained, and stuffed her ruined pocket down behind some palms. Then she dabbed at her stained dress with the napkin and her handkerchief. The skirt was really very wet, and she decided that it would not improve until it was dry. Until then she would try to keep well out of sight.

In the middle of the conservatory was a cluster of palms with rustic seats surrounding it. The foliage was very thick, but there was a clear space on the floor just beneath the lowest leaves, so she crawled under one of the seats, and stowed herself away there, quite confident of not being seen. She was sitting there still dabbing at her dress and thinking of all that had happened that day, when suddenly she saw two pairs of feet approaching her hiding place. A couple had come to sit on the seat in front of her. She recognised those worn dancing shoes and the hem of the flimsy skirt – it was her sister and Mr Horton. She sat still as a mouse.

"Miss Mannering," said Mr Horton in a low voice, "you must know that it was not for the pleasure of enter-

213

taining the entire troupe that I persuaded Mamma to extend the invitation tonight. You know that, do you not?"

Cecily said "yes" in such a low voice that Lexy could hardly hear it.

"You must have been aware of my feelings for you for some time – "

Suddenly Lexy stiffened. That had a very familiar ring. Why, it was from the proposal scene of "The False Marquess". Surely – surely – Mr Horton was not proposing to Cecily. But he was.

"Miss Mannering, before I make clear to you my purpose in asking you to listen to me, there is a question I must ask. It is about your profession. Would you miss the life of the theatre if you were to lose it? Could you leave your family, your career as an actress, the trouper's life?"

Cecily made a little gasping noise and then said, "Believe me, Mr Horton, my one wish is to leave the twoupe, to lead an ordinawy life, to be – to be a lady, not an actwess – and to live in a house – " She faltered and burst into tears.

"With me?" said Mr Horton breathlessly. "Oh, do not cry, my dearest dear. Do you mean – with me?"

Cecily sobbed her reply, and Lexy could not hear what it was, but Mr Horton continued, "Then, dearest Cecily, if those are your true feelings, will you, can you – may I implore you to do me the honour – the very great honour – " He faltered and could not find words.

"Of becoming my beloved and respected wife," prompted Lexy mechanically from "The False Marquess".

There was a horrified silence while she realised that she had given herself away. Then her hiding place among

214

the palms was discovered, and she was pulled out angrily by Cecily.

"How dare you! You detestable child. I shall never forgive you for this!"

"I am sorry," stammered Lexy, "but the ice cream melted – and I knew Mr Horton wanted to propose to you – "

Mr Horton suddenly doubled up with laughter.

"Thank you, little sister," he said, "for prompting me so neatly. Now can you prompt your sister in her reply?"

Cecily turned and faced him squarely. "I need no prompting," she said. "My answer is yes."

"But Cecily," gasped Lexy, "what will Papa say! He will never let you leave the troupe. He wants you to marry an actor, and stay with him always. You know that."

"As for Papa! He shall have no say in the matter," said Cecily with her eyes flashing. "Mr Horton and I will elope – without his permission – "

"I say, I say – " said Mr Horton, "when did we decide on that?"

"Be quiet," said Cecily firmly. "I have decided. We must elope. There is nothing else for it."

She turned to Lexy, "And *you* must help us."

CHAPTER 11

Found – An Actress

When Lexy woke up on Boxing Day she thought that she must still be dreaming. Surely it could not be true – that they had been to a ball the night before, and Mr Horton had proposed to Cecily and they were going to elope –

"Cecily, Cecily – " she nudged her sister to wake her, "pinch me, if you please, to see if I am dreaming." Cecily woke and immediately sat straight upright, wide awake. She looked at Lexy with wondering eyes.

"Yes, Lexy, and *you* pinch *me*. If I wemember what I think I wemember, then I too must be dweaming."

They solemnly pinched each other, but did not wake up.

"Then it must be twue – " cried Cecily. "Oh, Lexy, how wonderful – "

"Wonderful?" said Lexy. "I think it's terrible. Think in what a state Mamma and Papa will be! You're not truly going to elope are you?"

"Of course. What good would it do to ask Papa? You know he would say no. So it must be a wunaway mawwiage. Fwightfully womantic – " Cecily sighed and lay down again. "But we shall want a lot of help from you, Lexy. Can we depend on you?"

Lexy thought very hard. She did not want to grieve her parents, but on the other hand it did seem so very much the right thing for Cecily to do. It was not often that any one as kind and good and rich as Mr Horton proposed to an actress. And the theatre life certainly did not suit her – she would make such a good wife and hostess for someone like Mr Horton. And perhaps Mamma and Papa would become reconciled to the marriage when they saw what a good choice Cecily had made.

"Yes, Cecily. I will help you. What do you wish me to do?"

"I haven't weally thought yet. But I shall soon have a plan, never fear. Gwacious me, I've wead so many novels of elopements I ought to know the way to set about it."

"Well, at least wait until the Christmas show is over," pleaded Lexy. "The part of the fairy is so important, and there is no one who could take it instead of you."

"Perhaps I might wait until well into the New Year," mused Cecily. "After all, I must get together some semblance of a twousseau. And it would not look well to appear too eager – "

Lexy smiled to herself, remembering the scene she had overheard from her leafy hiding place. Then suddenly she remembered what day it was. It was Boxing Day, and the new show was to be put on. Romance must take second place. "Come, Cecily," she urged and leaped out of bed to dress by the blazing fire that had been lit by the maid while they slept.

All day Lexy had to keep reminding Cecily to pull herself together. She would find her standing in the wings,

217

staring into space, quite forgetting that she was supposed to be entering from the other side in a few minutes. They spent the day rehearsing odd patches of the play and putting final touches to the costumes. There was a lot of interest in the town in the new Christmas show, and the audiences poured into the theatre as soon as the doors were open. There were dozens of excited children, all in their best clothes being taken to the theatre for their Boxing Day treat. Joshua was rubbing his hands with satisfaction and thanking heaven for the change in their fortunes.

The play proved to be an enormous success. The children all loved the flying on wires and the gnome and fairy scenes, and Clem quite stole the hearts of the grown-ups as the changeling child. He piped away manfully all the evening, shaking his golden ringlets, dimpling his chubby cheeks and allowing large glistening tears to roll down his face whenever required.

Cecily looked more ravishing than ever as the fairy, and there was more of an ethereal air about her tonight than Lexy had ever noticed before. Perhaps it was the far-away look in her eyes that gave her performance that dreamy quality. Little did the audience realise that in her imagination the good fairy was presiding over Mr Horton's dinner table, complete with finger bowls and family silver.

The performance ended to tumultuous applause, and as the actors took their bows, gifts of fruit and flowers were handed up on to the stage. Lexy was surprised to receive something in a covered dish that felt very cold. She lifted the cover and looked inside. Standing up in a large mound of pink ice-cream was a card bearing the inscription, "*I trust that this will not melt too soon.*" In the dressing-room, she shared it with Clem, who, with tightly screwed up eyes because of the coldness of it, announced dreamily, "I think that heaven must be like this."

"Hush, Clem, that's wicked," said Seraphina.

Joshua burst into the dressing-room saying, "God bless you all, my dears! You've worked your hardest tonight and little Jamie has made his first appearance with great aplomb."

He surveyed them all proudly and slumped down into his chair in an exhausted manner.

"I am a fortunate man," he announced. "I have the dearest, cleverest family in the world. If Fate continues to smile in this way we shall be comfortable for the coming year. The manager has spoken of our remaining here as resident stock company. That would be pleasant, would it not?"

"Oh, Joshua," cried Seraphina, "how wonderful that would be! Not to have to travel for a while – "

"It is only a passing thought of his, my dear, but I think that if we continue to do a good season here it may bear fruit. And if we put on our very best shows and comport ourselves favourably it will, I am sure, persuade him to do so. Thanks be that my troupe are God-fearing and well-mannered. I've always known that refinement of behaviour was one of our chief assets. No scandal has ever been breathed about the members of our company – compare them with that wild gang of ruffians, the Wilings."

Lexy stole a glance at Cecily from under her lashes. If Cecily eloped with a member of the local aristocracy there would be plenty of scandal. But Cecily, quite oblivious, was staring at her reflection in the mirror with a faint smile on her lips, and had obviously not heard her father's remark.

"Cecily looks like a half-wit," said Clem reflectively, but Cecily did not even bother to slap him.

During the next few days she continued in this state of dreaminess and did not seem to be worrying about the situation in the least. It was Lexy who did all the worrying. A hundred times a day she imagined the distress of her mother and the fury of her father on discovering that Cecily was gone. And what would they do for another juvenile girl? The difficulty of finding a suitable one – another salary to pay out – Lexy's head spun, as she played the gnome and prompted and looked after Jamie and did all the dozens of jobs that made up her daily routine. Cecily was scheming to buy material for a new gown in which to be married.

"I always dweamed of being mawwied in white!" she confided in Lexy, "but I don't think that it would be quite cowwect for Gwetna Gween."

"Oh, Cecily!" gasped Lexy, "you're surely not being married at Gretna Green?"

There had been a scene of a runaway marriage in "Lady Fanny's Elopement" so Lexy knew all about it.

"But – by a blacksmith – how could you?"

"Oh, we shall weturn to the Hall and have another ceremony in the village church, as soon as the pawents are pacified," said Cecily.

Lexy thought that was a very good thing.

The fairy play continued to be very popular, and its run was extended by another week.

"After that," announced Joshua, "the management wishes us to vary our bill between Shakespeare and modern pieces. We shall commence with 'Romeo and Juliet'."

Cecily groaned, for Juliet was her longest part, then she caught Lexy's eye and smiled a serene smile.

"How soon will that be, Papa?" she asked innocently.

"Three weeks ahead," said Joshua.

"Cecily," said Lexy some time later, "what will you do? You cannot leave us stranded with no Juliet!"

"Mamma can play it. She always did before I weturned – And a gweat deal better than I have ever done, or so I hear tell fwom evewyone."

On the following Sunday Cecily had arranged to meet Mr Horton to discuss their plans. It was a luxury for the company to spend a Sunday resident in one place. In the morning the whole family went to church, including Jamie who sang loudly long after the choir and the rest of the congregation had finished. Returning to the Red Lion with Jamie on his father's back, Cecily and Lexy walking primly in front of their parents and Clem skipping along ahead, they might have been any family in the world, thought Lexy, until she heard an excited whisper as they passed another family.

"Look, Mamma, look, Papa – there go the play-actors – "

After their luncheon, Joshua and Seraphina retired to rest during the afternoon, and before they went Cecily said casually, "I think that Lexy and I will take the air a little. It is a nice bwight afternoon."

"Will you take Clem too?" asked Seraphina.

"Don't want to go," said Clem.

"No, Mamma, not if he does not wish to come; he dwags his feet so."

"You would like it when you were out, Clem."

"Don't want to walk, want to ride. I'll come if I can bring my horse."

221

"No! No!" exclaimed Cecily. "It's tedious pushing you all the while on that howwid animal!"

"Then, Clem, you must play quietly by yourself."

The two girls heaved a sigh of relief.

As they went out of the house Lexy felt as guilty as if she were the culprit.

"Where are you meeting him?" she whispered hoarsely.

"By the wiverside," replied Cecily. "Please will you walk behind us just far enough not to be able to hear – well, that is – just far enough not to disturb us, and yet seem as if you are with us."

"Yes," sighed Lexy. "But do not stay long, now will you? And tell him you cannot go until after 'Romeo and Juliet'."

Down among the bare boughs of the willow trees on the riverside was the handsome figure of Mr Horton. He greeted them both eagerly, and Lexy fell behind as they paced up and down, up and down along the tow-path. The winter dusk fell early, and soon she was shivering and having to blow into her mittens to keep her fingers warm. Four o'clock struck on all the town clocks.

"Cecily," she called, "we'd best go home. Mamma and Papa will be waking."

"Yes, yes. In a minute."

Lexy surveyed the grey stretch of the river, and the roof tops of Marlingford in their grey evening shroud and went all through her lines for "The Enchanted Glade" and then started on "Romeo and Juliet", doing everybody's lines. At last she could hear goodbyes being said.

"Goodbye, dear heart. Do not neglect our awwangements. Until two weeks fwom now – "

"Yes, my dear. And do not fret. It will all be well."

"Come *along*, Cecily!" urged Lexy and took her sister firmly by the arm. "They will think you have eloped already!"

She had almost to drag her sister away, for she kept turning to blow one last kiss to Mr Horton. They sped home through the darkening streets where the lamplighters were lighting the lamps with their long poles, and the muffin-men were going their rounds, ringing their bells and shouting their wares.

"We'll buy some for tea," announced Cecily. "It will be an excuse for being out so long."

"Cecily!" said Lexy anxiously, "what have you planned for two Sundays ahead?"

"That is when we are going – We shall meet just as today – but – but you will weturn alone, Lexy, dear."

Cecily squeezed her hand affectionately.

"Do not fwet. It will be fwightfully pleasant when I am mawwied. You shall come to stay with me, and I shall be able to buy you new dwesses. I shall be able to buy us *all* new dwesses – if only Mamma and Papa will not be too cwoss with me. You will persuade them it is for the best, will you not?"

"I'll try," said Lexy. "But I know that Papa will be angry."

When they arrived back at the inn everything looked wonderfully safe and cosy and homely, and they toasted the muffins in front of the big fire in their parents' room, and Seraphina brewed some tea on the spirit-stove.

"Do not go away – " suddenly whispered Lexy very quietly in Cecily's ear. Cecily looked round the room, and

223

Lexy saw that she was fighting a battle inside herself. Her blue eyes filled.

"I must!" she said, and taking Jamie on to her lap hid her face in his fluffy down of curls.

The next fortnight passed so smoothly and pleasantly that Lexy would have been able to forget all about the pending crisis if it had not been for Cecily's frantic sewing and reorganising of her wardrobe.

"Such activity!" exclaimed Seraphina. "I declare, one would think you were preparing your trousseau!"

Cecily blushed, but Seraphina went on quite calmly, "I must say, though, it is a blessing to be in one place long enough to catch up with such things."

Joshua was full of plans for the new season and was discussing who should play which parts.

"If only I could *tell* him," thought Lexy in agony, "then he could look for another girl – "

"He'll find another, never fear," said Cecily when Lexy said this to her. "A dozen or more, should he so wish. I am doing the pwofession a kindness by leaving it – it means work for one more actwess."

The fateful Sunday drew nearer and nearer. Lexy was much more nervous than Cecily.

"But, Cecily – " she said, "how am I to tell them that you have gone? I cannot just return and say, 'Cecily has gone.' They would not believe me – they would think me mad."

"I will write them a note," said Cecily confidently, "explaining evewything. And you shall give it to them."

Lexy gulped and tried not to imagine the scene.

The last performance of "The Enchanted Glade" on the Saturday night was an enormous success. The audience would not let them go and showered flowers down on them from the gallery. Joshua was deeply gratified, and Lexy was having to fight back the tears, thinking that this was Cecily's last appearance on the stage, and nobody knew. But Cecily herself did not care. She danced back to their little strip of a dressing-room and tore off her frock, leaving it on the floor in a heap. She wiped off her make-up saying, "There – that's an end of that wretched stuff."

She picked up her make-up box and handed it to Lexy.

"This is for you, darling child. Your little, old cigar box is so shabby."

"Thank you," said Lexy miserably, but could not feel really pleased about the gift.

"I wonder," said Joshua entering the dressing-room, "if tomorrow we should rehearse for 'Romeo and Juliet'. It is a long time since it has been in the bill. Do you think you remember it, daughter?"

"Why, yes, Papa," said Cecily with wide-eyed innocence. "I am sure I wemember it *quite* as well as I shall need."

"I will take your word, but do not let me down, me girl, for so much depends on these next few weeks."

Lexy shuddered at Joshua's grave tone.

When they went to bed that night Lexy was feeling very miserable, but Cecily was as gay as a lark. She kept leaping out of bed to add one more object to the carpet bag that was the only luggage she was taking.

"A portmanteau would look obvious," she said. "And besides, I have so few things that are worth taking."

At last she settled down and fell asleep, but Lexy cried quietly to herself for some long time. When she awoke

225

Cecily was already up and pattering round the room in her bare feet.

The day followed the pattern of the previous Sundays. They went to church in the morning, and Lexy hardly dared to pray, for she felt so guilty. At lunch she could eat nothing, although Cecily was eating ravenously, with a high colour in her cheeks and shining eyes.

"You're sickening for something, my lamb," said Seraphina. "I hope it's not this unpleasant colic that is going around. I am not feeling too well myself. I think I shall lie down this afternoon. Why do you not do the same, Lexy?"

Lexy gulped.

"Oh, all the child needs is a bweath of fwesh air. We'll go for our constitutional this afternoon, Lexy."

"I feel ill too," announced Clem. "I've got scarlatina, and I'll probably die."

"Nonsense," said Joshua. "You've eaten too good a dinner to die yet awhile, my man."

"You'll be sorry when I'm dead," said Clem darkly.

Joshua continued to sit by the fire in the inn dining-room looking over his part for "Romeo and Juliet", while Seraphina went to lie down. Lexy and Cecily went to their room and put on their cloaks and bonnets. Cecily skipped into her mother's darkened room and kissed her on the forehead.

"Au revoir, Mamma," she said. "I hope you will soon feel better."

She picked up her carpet bag, and with Lexy following behind she went into the dining-room, keeping the bag under her cloak. She bent and kissed her father on the forehead in silence, but he was so deep in his part that he did not even notice. On the threshold of the hotel Cecily did not even look back.

"I do not understand you," said Lexy wonderingly. "How *could* anyone be so calm, when running away from home?"

"I am not wunning *away* fwom home – " said Cecily. "We have never had a home, you know. I am wunning *to* my home." And she increased her speed along the deserted Sunday streets.

On the bridge over the river stood a small, but smartly-painted carriage.

"Isn't it beautiful!" exclaimed Cecily. "Is is his *own*, his vewy own. It does not belong to his family."

Mr Horton leaped out as soon as he saw them approach. He kissed both of them affectionately and looked for a long time into Cecily's eyes before saying:

"If you have any regrets, realise them now and turn back. I shall not reproach you."

"Turn back?" cried Cecily. "Never! Why," she laughed a little tremulously, "why, here is my twousseau!" She held up the pathetic carpet bag that looked so ridiculous that they all burst out laughing. But Lexy was so strung-up that her laughter turned to tears, and she buried her face in Cecily's cloak.

"Do not cry," said Mr Horton kindly, "or we shall feel we must take you with us – But wait and see what times we shall have when Cecily and I have our own establishment, and you are our first guest of honour."

"Oh, Lexy, before I forget," Cecily plunged her hand into her reticule and produced a letter, "this is for Papa. I have told him that you did not help us willingly, just so that you shall not get involved with my disgwace. Now, goodbye, dear little Lexy. I must have been a sad twial to you while I have been with the twoupe – I pwomise to make it up to you fwom now on." She kissed Lexy affectionately. "You are a dear, good child – "

Mr Horton kissed her also, saying, "You thought on first sight that I was a robber. I am very sorry for stealing your sister. Please forgive me – "

The tears were rolling down Lexy's face uncontrollably. She wanted to say that she hoped they would be happy, that she knew they were doing the right thing, that she would try to persuade her parents of this – but she could only sob and sniff and try to smile. Then they got into the carriage and it rolled off, with Cecily leaning out of the window to wave until it rounded the corner. Lexy stared after it until the sound of the horses' hooves had completely died away, and then she put her head down on the parapet of the bridge and sobbed aloud. She stayed there until it was so dark and cold that she could stand it no longer, and then, holding the fateful letter as though it were burning hot, she made for the Red Lion. She looked into the dining-room as she passed. Joshua was dozing by the fire. She put her head round her mother's door and was met with a miserable snuffle and, "Oh, close the door, child, I've got such a cold of the head. So suddenly it has come, too!"

Lexy walked round the room she had shared with Cecily. It looked so cold and deserted now – with all Cecily's favourite trinkets missing. The letter had still to be delivered – Clem poked his head round the door.

"Where's Cecily? She promised to give me rides on Dobbin today, and she hasn't!"

Lexy said, "Go and wash your hands for tea. But don't disturb Mamma. She's poorly – "

She went into the dining-room and said timidly, "Papa – "

Joshua sat up stretching and yawning. "Ah – tea-time," he said. "Are we to have it upstairs or here?"

"Mamma is feeling poorly," said Lexy. "We'd best have it down here. Papa – "

"Ring the bell then, child."

Lexy did so.

"Papa!" she began again. "There is something I want to say."

"Why, goodness gracious me!" said Joshua in mock horror, "I have forgotten your pocket-money. How could such an important financial consideration escape my notice! See, I have added some interest as compensation." He laughed jovially and pressed three pennies into her hand.

"I did not mean – " she began.

"No, no, child. You did right to remind me. One should be as conscientious in small transactions as in large. Think no more of it."

The waiter entered, and Joshua said, "Might we have a pot of tea in here, if you please? Usually we brew our own, I am aware, but my good lady is indisposed."

At this moment Clem came in pushing his horse.

"Papa, Papa," he cried, "will *you* give me rides? That horrid Cecily promised, but now I can't find her."

"Can't find her? – She must be somewhere in the hotel – What is she doing? Prinking in her mirror as usual, I'll be bound. Go, fetch her, Lexy!"

"I cannot, Papa," said Lexy in a tiny voice, holding out the letter. "She has gone – "

"*Gone*?" Joshua rolled the word out so that it seemed to fill the room, and Lexy could not help thinking of his scene as Shylock in "The Merchant of Venice" when he discovered his daughter's disappearance. Joshua took hold of her by her shoulders and shook her. "What is the meaning of this? What are you talking of?"

"P – please, Papa – read this."

He took the note and read it, and all the colour drained from his face. He seemed suddenly to look a very old man. He sank into his chair.

"Eloped," he said dully.

He turned fiercely on Lexy again.

"Who is this scoundrel?" he demanded.

"Does she not say, Papa?"

"No, she does not. And you do not need to pretend that you are ignorant of who it is!" A sudden thought struck him. "It's not – it's not that young puppy Courtney Stanton?"

"Oh no, Papa. It's not an actor. It's a gentleman."

"For heaven's sake, tell me *who*." He started to shake her again.

"It's Mr Horton – "

"And who might *he* be – the villain – "

"Do – do stop shaking me, Papa. I am trying to tell you."

He let her go, rather shamefaced.

"Do you remember when we played at Oldcastle, and there was that very rowdy gallery, and a gentleman in a box stood up and shouted at them? It is he – "

Joshua was dumbfounded.

"But – but she doesn't know him – "

"Yes, she does, Papa. It was to his parents' house that we went on Christmas night. And she originally met him at the Pagetts', and he is very nice, Papa, and very rich, and I'm sure that you and Mamma will like him."

Joshua was suddenly furious again.

"Like him, indeed! The pair of them need not think that we shall have further dealings with them. The scandal of it – "

Joshua slapped his hand to his brow and paced the room like an angry lion.

"And just at this time when it is so important for our

231

name to be well thought of in the town. And with one of the local quality – Oh, what a daughter! What a daughter! Why, why, *why* – did she not ask your mother and me if she might marry him?"

"Because she knew you'd say no. You *would* have, wouldn't you, Papa?"

"Yes, I should have said no," fumed Joshua. "We are a trouping family, and I am proud of it. I do not wish my daughters to marry to better themselves – they should stay with the troupe – and pull their weight. Not gallivant off with rich squires without so much as a by-your-leave. It's scandalous – scandalous. It will ruin us in Marlingford."

Lexy was nearly in tears again.

"*I* will not leave the troupe – ever, Papa!" she said. "I do not wish to be a married lady. I shall stay with you and Mamma always – "

"*You* – said Joshua witheringly. "Tcha!"

Lexy hung her head miserably.

They had both forgotten that Clem was still in the room. He was sitting astride his wooden horse listening open-mouthed. Now he enquired with interest, "Has Cecily done something bad?"

"Silence – " thundered Joshua. "Never mention that name again in my presence."

"What, Cecily?" went on Clem. "Mustn't I mention Cecily's name again? Then what shall I call her? Shall I have to call her 'Sis' like Jamie does?"

"Hush, hush, Clem – " said Lexy. "You do not understand."

Joshua sank into his chair again.

"I shall have to tell your mother – what will she feel?

She will have to play Juliet tomorrow – and she is ill already. Oh, Cecily, Cecily – " He hid his face in his hands.

"You said not to mention that name," Clem reminded him.

Lexy picked him up and carried him bodily from the room.

"Papa is unhappy. Do not vex him. Run up to our room – to my room and sit there until I come to you."

"Is Papa crying? I didn't think papas did – "

"No, of course not. He is – worried!"

"Oh – " Clem lost interest in the subject. "Do you think he'll give me rides after tea?"

"No!" Lexy almost shouted. "I don't think anyone will be able to give you rides for a long, long time."

She went back into the dining-room just as the waiter entered with the tea. As soon as she had departed she said timidly to Joshua: "Am I to tell Mamma?"

"I shall tell her – " Joshua walked from the room with his head bowed. Lexy followed very softly and stood outside the doors of her mother's room. She heard her father's angry voice, and then her mother's sobs. Among them she heard the words, "My daughter – a wicked man like that – "

Without another thought Lexy ran into her mother's room, and knelt by the side of her bed, "Mamma – " she cried, "do not be unhappy for Cecily! He is *not* a wicked man – he is good and kind and he loves Cecily. He did not take her away against her will. At the last minute he begged her to change her mind if she felt unsure."

"So *you* knew about it – " moaned Seraphina. "And you told us nothing – Oh, Lexy, how could you treat us so? Both daughters deceiving us – "

"But, Mamma, if only you knew Mr Horton – I know you would think as I do. He is very rich and can give Cecily all the pretty things she's always wanted. His father and mother are a Sir and a Lady, but he is only a mister. They live in a great big house – the one we went to on Christmas night – and he is the gentleman who stood up in the box that night at Oldcastle, and shouted out to the gallery to be quiet. Do you not remember? You admired him then – and so did Papa."

"But – to run off with Cecily – Oh, the dear thing – and we shall never see her again!"

"Yes, you will, Mamma, if Papa will allow it, that is. They want us to go and stay with them whenever we can. That will be lovely, Mamma, now won't it? And Cecily will be so much happier. She hated the stage, you know – " Lexy was comforting her mother just as Cecily had comforted her, a few hours previously.

"But what about tomorrow?" wailed Seraphina. "I shall have to play Juliet – it's nearly a year since I played it. And since Cecily returned and I've not had to play all the romantic parts, I've – I've aged so much. I've put on weight – I'll never get into the dresses – Oh, Joshua, what are we to do?"

"You shall play Juliet tomorrow. It hardly matters what you wear. Our reputation in Marlingford will be gone. We can look forward to another year of the barns and fit-ups – while Cecily, whose fault it is, queens it in her own mansion," said Joshua bitterly.

"But why is it a disgrace for an actress to marry well?" demanded Lexy.

"It's the *eloping*," groaned Seraphina, "that is so

scandalous. It is so unlike Cecily. She always wanted to be so correct – "

"She always wanted to be a lady," argued Lexy, "and now she will be one."

"Are his parents *really* a Sir and a Lady – what? Horton? Why, yes, that is a well-known name in these parts – mill-owners, I believe." Seraphina stopped crying and a speculative look came into her eye. "I wonder what he is worth – "

"Worth? He is very worthy, Mamma!" Lexy assured her.

"In money, I mean. Several thousands a year, I'll be bound. Is he handsome, Lexy?"

"Oh, yes, Mamma – as handsome as – as handsome as Papa – only younger, of course – "

Seraphina gave a little half-laughing sob and put her arms round Lexy.

"Funny child – we still have you."

Lexy thought that this was a much nicer reaction than her father's.

"Yes, Mamma," she said, "and I will never leave you."

At this Seraphina broke down and cried so much that Joshua had to go and fetch some brandy and smelling-salts for her.

The rest of Sunday was terrible. Alternately Seraphina and Joshua wept and stormed, and Clem would not be quiet and kept making tactless remarks until Lexy put him to bed. Seraphina's cold got worse and worse until what with that and with crying, she was in a state of extreme and miserable dampness. Both of them had fits of turning on Lexy and blaming her for not warning them of Cecily's elopement – and then she would tell them more about Mr Horton's house and his parents and his carriage, and they would calm down a little. Then Seraphina would remember that she had to play next day, and off she would start once more. Then Joshua would say that he never wished to see Cecily again, and Seraphina would say that he was heartless.

By bedtime Lexy was so exhausted that she just fell into bed without washing – and then was cold all night because she missed the warmth of her sister beside her.

She had a terrible dream that she had to go on to play Juliet and found herself riding round the stage on Clem's wooden horse, and all the audience laughed at her, but at the back of the theatre she could see Cecily and Mr Horton flying about on the flying wires that had been used in "The Enchanted Glade".

She was awakened by someone shaking her. As she opened her eyes and realised that it was morning, her father, leaning over her in his wrapper said, "Alexandra! Your mother's voice has completely left her. You will have to play Juliet tonight!"

Still half asleep Lexy said quite calmly, "Nonsense. That's only what I dreamt."

Joshua slapped her lightly on the cheek. "Lexy! Wake up. You're not dreaming. This is true. Your mother's cold has gone to her chest and throat. She will never have a voice by tonight, and it would be madness for her to leave her bed. She cannot utter a sound. Do you understand?"

Lexy sat up slowly, unable to believe her ears.

"Papa, are you joking? *Me* play Juliet?"

Her father shouted angrily.

"Yes! It's the worst misfortune that has ever befallen the troupe – but there is no help for it. It's you or Gertrude

236

Tollerton. One's as bad as the other. She at least is an actress, but she's old enough to be grandmother to Romeo – and at all events she'd never fit the costumes. But on you, they can be tucked and altered. You know the lines, of course?"

"Why, yes, Papa – but – but the audience will laugh – "

"If they do," said Joshua grimly, "I'll – I'll – " he searched for the worst threat he could think of. "I'll send you back to school! Come now. Get up. I know it's early, but I must rehearse you all day. Goodness knows what sort of a show it will be – but we are finished in Marlingford, that I know already – "

He banged angrily out of the room.

Lexy lay quite still, wondering if it was all a dream. But no – it was true. It was really happening. *She* – Alexandra Mannering, thirteen years old, with protruding teeth, was to play Juliet that night! With a cry of horror she leaped out of bed, flung her cloak round her and ran in to see her mother. Seraphina mouthed a silent greeting to her, her eyes glazed and streaming with cold.

"Voice gone – completely – could never play tonight – " she whispered pathetically.

Lexy gazed at her, stricken, and found herself whispering too in sympathy.

"But, Mamma, you *must* – I can't play Juliet."

"Yes, dear, you must. It's the only thing. You know it all."

"But *me*, Mamma – I'm only a child!"

"It is not unusual. Many of the great actresses have played Juliet at your age."

237

"But I'm not a great actress. I shall ruin it – they will laugh at me – "

"Oh, if only Cecily would come back!" gasped Seraphina. "But get dressed at once, child, and go over to the theatre quickly. Your father will wish to work with you – and ask Mrs Tollerton to alter the dresses. Tell her how ill I feel and ask if she will be good enough to help keep an eye on Jamie. Say I am sorry to be of so little use. If there is much sewing to do, Lexy, I can do it if someone brings it over here to me – "

Lexy was surprised to see that the whole thing was completely settled, that she had got to play Juliet that night. In a dazed condition she washed and dressed and went over to the theatre. From the expressions of unbelieving horror on the faces of the rest of the company she knew that they had already heard. Courtney Stanton kept looking from her to Gertrude Tollerton and back again, as though trying to decide which was the lesser of the two evils. Then he shook his head despairingly and walked into the wings. Joshua was in deep conversation with the theatre manager, who was looking very dubious. Then suddenly a light dawned on his face – "We will turn this to our advantage," he said smiling. "I will get out new bills – a child prodigy – Juliet at the age that Shakespeare intended her to be – yes, I see it all now – "

He hurried off delightedly.

Joshua, though relieved that the manager had taken it so well, was still in a very bad temper.

"Well," he said in a surly manner to the company, "let us make the best of a bad job. I assure you I will find us a juvenile girl as soon as it is humanly possible. I have already written to London on the subject. Now, let us start to run through. This will be just for moves and business. I will coach Lexy privately this afternoon when no-one else need attend. Now, let us begin."

Lexy was as nervous as though it were her first morning in a strange company. She knew the lines perfectly, and she could remember exactly how Cecily had delivered them, and exactly how her mother used to do them. She decided to copy her mother and did so in every inflection – but the effect, coming from such a young girl, was comical and the company had to hide their smiles. Lexy could see this and was miserably unhappy. She stopped in the middle of a speech – and said brokenly, "It's of no use, Papa, I shall never be able to do it."

Joshue immediately flew into a frenzy. "Carry on, if you please," he shouted. "I do not ask you to act. Just say the lines and I'll be satisfied."

For the rest of the morning she just recited the lines parrot-fashion, and so did everybody else.

"We shall pack the theatre, I am convinced," said Joshua sarcastically.

Lexy flushed at her father's unkindness but knew that most of it was caused by his unhappiness about Cccily.

When the rehearsal broke up for luncheon Gertrude Tollerton took her to try on the costumes. They were all much too big for her and eventually Mrs Tollerton decided that she should only wear two different gowns, and she fitted them on her, sticking pins into her heedless of her surprised squeaks.

"Don't fret, deary," she said kindly. "You'll not do badly. In the eyes of an audience a child can do no wrong on the stage. They think it clever even if they only walk on.

239

And look at the way they love young Clem. And he's no actor as we know!"

"But he's pretty," said Lexy miserably, "and look at me!"

She certainly looked a quaint picture in the mirror in a gown that hung on her like a sack and her face white and peaked with fright.

"A little paint will soon improve you. And we'll curl your hair and pin that fringe back, and you'll not look unlike your poor, dear sister.'

"You say that as though she were dead – " observed Lexy. "She's only married." And she sighed to think of all the trouble that Cecily had caused.

Lexy only had time for a bowl of soup and a bun in a coffee shop before she was due to go through the part with her father. The set was up by this time, and he made her go through the entire part, line by line, with him – telling her what it meant and how he wished it said. Lexy discovered that she had misunderstood the meaning of many of the lines for years, and it was difficult for her to think of them in any other way. Her father began to be a little better tempered, so earnestly was he trying to prepare her to play the part.

"Do not imitate your mother, do not, certainly, imitate your sister – they are older, and what is right for them to do in the part is not right for you. Your only hope is to play it simply and from the heart – " He broke off despairingly. "Though how a child like you is to be expected to portray these deep emotions, I do not know – "

"I'll try, Papa," said Lexy, wide-eyed with fear.

She tried as hard as she knew how. But her voice

sounded shrill and piping – and she knew that her movements were awkward and coltish.

"Not bad," said Joshua, in a resigned way, after five
hours' solid work. "Now, go away and think about all I
have said. You know the lines well – that is the greatest
comfort. Have a bite to eat, and come back to the theatre
in good time. Stanton may want a few final words with
you."

Lexy had not got the heart to eat. She wandered
aimlessly round the cold, dark streets of Marlingford in a
state of blind panic. At one instant she thought quite seriously of throwing herself under the wheels of a carriage in
the High Street, so that she would be injured and not have
to go on. But then she reflected that her parents had suffered
enough already. And all the time she felt that if only she
could discover some magic charm, some trick, some secret
– she would be able to play the part. After all – she had
had a lot of acting experience – and Juliet was only supposed
to be a young girl – But it was so difficult to imagine being
in love with Courtney Stanton – and going off and marrying
him secretly – just like Cecily and Mr Horton.

Suddenly her heart leapt – of course – that was the
idea – she must look as Cecily had looked lately, speak as
she had spoken in that brave exultant fashion. She must try
to look at Romeo in the way that Cecily had looked at Mr
Horton, softly, trustingly – She quickened her pace, smiling
to herself, and then tried to do the little mysterious half-
smile of Cecily's while she had been planning her elopement. Yes – that was the idea – But how was she to do the
highly emotional suicide scene in the tomb – She must think
of the most harrowing things she had ever known – Jamie's
illness – Cecily's departure even – Yes, she must relate it

all to her own experience and observation. Papa had not thought to tell her that, but suddenly she knew that it was the only hope for her. She turned back towards the theatre – and for the first time in her life the evening before her meant more than the mere routine of going through the show and packing up again afterwards. There seemed to be something that she wanted to do, something she wanted to say, something she wanted to *impart* – It was because of this discovery of hers that Juliet was not just a long and difficult classical rôle that was a test of the skill of any actress – She was a person who had behaved very much like Cecily – and Lexy had suddenly found that she wanted to show everybody just how it was. It was a strange sensation and made her head feel as though it were bursting with thoughts and activity. Perhaps she had never really *thought* before – But, of course, Juliet was a more sensible and serious person than Cecily – there must be none of that pretty vanity and pertness.

Outside the theatre the new bills were up.

A SPECIAL ATTRACTION
for the
CITIZENS OF MARLINGFORD.

TO-NIGHT
in this Theatre
the first appearance on any stage in this rôle
of
THE CHILD PRODIGY
ALEXANDRA MANNERING
(daughter of Joshua Mannering)
as
JULIET
in
THE TRAGEDY OF 'ROMEO AND JULIET'

Scenes include a square in Verona, the palace
of Capulet, the palace of Montague, a ghostly
tomb – to be followed by a comic burlesque.

Lexy had seen her name on the bills as long as she could
remember, but tonight it gave her a thrill of anticipation –
half pleasant, half terrifying.

As if in a dream, she went to the place in the dressing-
room that had been Cecily's and allowed Mrs Tollerton to
do her make-up and dress her as though she were a doll.

Gertrude Tollerton was worried by her strange look.
"Now do not panic. There'll be someone on the book the
entire time. You've only to look to the prompt side – and
we all know your lines backwards, so we can help you out."

"Thank you – " said Lexy, looking at her reflection
in surprise. Certainly a touch of colour on her cheeks and
lips was a great improvement. Her teeth did not seem so

much in evidence. And without her fringe she looked years older – and very much like Cecily, as Mrs Tollerton had said. Clem came in and looked gravely at her.

"You don't look such a fright!" he said.

Courtney Stanton kept popping in with fresh bits of advice. "It might be best," he said, "if you were to cut to the cue lines of all your speeches – just give the skeleton of them – "

"No," said Lexy, looking straight at him, "I shall say all the lines."

He shrugged his shoulders and looked offended. Her father came in and seemed quite surprised.

"Delightful, child – you look delightful," and in a low voice said to Mrs Tollerton, "You have done wonders, dear lady. She looks quite classical. Do you know, she is more *striking* than her sister – "

Now Lexy's determination began to flag. The palms of her hands were wet, and she felt very sick. The orchestra could be heard tuning up.

"Ought I to go and call the five minutes?" she asked her father. It was her job usually to call warning of the time to all the company.

"Mercy me, you are the leading lady tonight! Clem shall do it."

Then in at the dressing-room door came her mother – wrapped up in a cocoon of mufflers and shawls.

"Seraphina!" exclaimed Joshua. "How dare you leave your bed!"

"I had to come," whispered Seraphina hoarsely, "to see this dear child perform. I *could* not stay away. The manager is giving me a nice warm box. Do well, my lamb." She kissed her lovingly. "I am sorry to be the cause of this ordeal. But you are a real little trooper, and I know you will not let us down."

Her mother's words warmed her, but the worst time was to come, when everyone else had to go for the opening of the play and she had to wait until the third scene before appearing. Then the silence backstage was so deep that she could hear every word that was spoken and every footfall. She could hear her first scene approaching and went and stood in the wings. Everyone there made silent gestures of surprise and approval at her appearance.

"It's a packed house for the prodigy," Barney Fidgett whispered. "They've all heard about Cecily, and have come to see what her sister's like. Don't disappoint 'em, me child."

As the curtain went up on the scene in which Juliet first appears, Lexy was breathing as heavily as though she had been running.

" 'Where's the girl? What, Juliet!' " came her cue from Mrs Tollerton as the Nurse. And she was on, saying quite gaily, and in perfect control of herself,

" 'How now! who calls?' "

This was an easy scene and made no tax on her acting abilities but the audience applauded enthusiastically at the end of it.

"They like you, lambkin," said Mrs Tollerton with an approving pat.

Lexy was nervous before the ballroom scene, because it was her first scene with Courtney. She knew he was a difficult and selfish actor – he did not seem to radiate waves of sympathy to her as Gertrude Tollerton did. But in this scene she was thinking hard of Cecily and Mr Horton –

245

remembering them at the dance on Christmas night – how Cecily had looked and spoken.

And then came the balcony scene, the dream and nightmare of every actress. As she climbed the rough ladder backstage, her heart was beating like a drum. And then she glided forward, and, leaning her elbow on the balcony, rested her cheek in the palm of her hand. The audience was a blur of pale moons arranged in rows – "white-upturned wondering eyes of mortals" as Romeo was that instant saying. There had been a ripple of sentimental approval as she had appeared, and now as she started to speak, there was that silence – that glorious silence of an audience hanging on the words of an actor – the sort of silence that Joshua sometimes commanded. Lexy suddenly felt so powerful that it seemed to her almost as if she were singing in an enormous operatic tone – and yet she could hear the rise and fall of her own clear yet childish voice. When the applause burst out at the end she felt completely exhausted, but there was still the greater part of the play remaining. She sat on a chair in the wings while the next scene was in progress and they brought her a glass of brandy and water.

"Splendid, my darling, splendid," Joshua was urging her, "but keep it up!"

"It's so – exhausting," gasped Lexy. "I feel as if I've been climbing a mountain."

Joshua looked at her as if they shared a secret. "It *is* exhausting, isn't it?" he agreed and then he appeared delighted with her. "Keep it up, child. You shall have whatever reward you ask for."

"Do you mean that, Papa? Then please – will you be friends with Cecily?"

"Anything, anything – "

All the rest of the play she was hardly conscious when she was off-stage – there was nothing but the joys and sorrows of poor Juliet and the terrible awakening in the tomb to find Romeo lying dead at her side. Then she was Seraphina looking at the fevered face of Jamie when they were at Scanchester – and Cecily if something terrible had happened to Mr Horton, and Lexy trying to show the audience exactly how it would be, and Juliet, all those years ago in Verona.

Watching this particular play on previous occasions she had always wondered how the people playing the parts of Romeo and Juliet could lie perfectly still for so long at the end of the play, while all the others came on and discovered them and tied up the ends of the plot. But tonight she found no difficulty in it. She was so exhausted that she felt almost as though she *were* dead – and it was like heaven to be able to lie perfectly still and relaxed and to know that it was all over. She had to be lifted up and fanned with Mrs Tollerton's apron before she could collect herself properly. The company crowded round her, congratulating her, kissing her, patting her, and in their eyes a new light – not the patronising, kindly, rather contemptuous look to which she had been used, but something surprised and a little respectful. Then Joshua was waving them into some sort of line for the curtain call, and the heavy plush curtain was sweeping up – and there was the audience again, still clapping and smiling, and Lexy being led forward by her father.

"Well done, little ha'p'orth," shouted a rough voice from the gallery.

Lexy looked up and curtsied gravely, and the house

roared its approval. In the stage box Seraphina was leaning out so far that Lexy was afraid she might fall. Tears were streaming down her face – and she was mopping them up with a sodden handkerchief, coughing and sneezing and clutching her shawl up to her neck, but looking radiantly happy. "Bless you," she was mouthing dumbly to Lexy.

In front of the whole house Joshua put his arms round his daughter and embraced her.

"Was I all right, Papa?" said Lexy, still quite dazed.

"Dear child, dear child – " he said softly, "I may have lost a daughter but I have found an actress."

And Lexy's heart lifted and sang.